Dee's mouth was moving, saying something, but I couldn't hear her because, at that point, the front door was flung open and the boys from Farnsworth Prep came swarming in.

I forgot what day or year it was. I almost forgot my own name.

For there, spearheading the right-front flank, was the boy I'd been dreaming about all my life. Well, since I hit puberty, anyway.

He looked at me. I looked at him. Two strangers across a crowded room.

And then, in my imagination, the strains of the overture to Tchaikovsky's *Romeo and Juliet* swelled and filled the haunted halls of Miss Minsham's Academy for Girls.

BEBE FAAS RICE has written a number of magazine articles and short stories, one of which, "The Man Who Killed the King," was selected for the anthology, *Julie Nixon Eisenhower's Favorite Stories for Children*. Ms. Rice is married to a Marine major general and has one son, John. She is an amateur historian, a mad antique-er and the owner of Max, "a dog of little brain but great charm."

BEBE FAAS RICE

Boy Crazy

Keepsake FROM CROSSWINDS

CROSSWINDS

New York • Toronto • Sydney
Auckland • Manila

To Duff and John—
for never was heard a discouraging word

First publication July 1988

ISBN 0-373-88027-8

Dear Reader:

Welcome to our line of teen romances, Keepsake from Crosswinds. Here, as you can see, the focus is on the relationship between girls and boys, while the setting, story and the characters themselves contribute the variety and excitement you demand.

We hope that you are also enjoying our other novels under the Crosswinds logo. These lively stories featuring young characters in contemporary situations are bound to hold your interest.

As always, your comments and suggestions are welcome. They help us to keep Crosswinds where it belongs—at the very top of your reading list!

Nancy Jackson

Nancy Jackson
Senior Editor
CROSSWINDS

Chapter One

Everything that happened in the fall of my sophomore year—attending a posh boarding school for girls, launching a no-holds-barred feud with Raquel Finnerty and falling madly in love with the boy of my dreams—was the direct result of Great-Uncle William's death.

His passing came as a surprise to all of us. Granted, he was eighty-two years old, but he was still full of pepper and vinegar. And besides, as Dad always said, "That old grinch is too mean to die."

As fate would have it, neither illness nor old age carried Uncle Will off to his Great Reward. The proper term for what happened would probably be "death by misadventure."

It seems Uncle Will was gunning down the halls of the Smiling Hills Nursing Home in his motorized wheelchair, bent on overtaking and ramming a rival, when he veered off course, bounced down two flights of winding stairs and wound up in a spectacular finale against the front wall of the reception area which, unfortunately for Uncle Will, was made of polished Vermont granite.

Few mourned his untimely demise. I heard later that his neighbors in the F Wing of Smiling Hills actually cracked out their best bottles of brandy and champagne, hidden in shoe boxes and under beds, and toasted his departure with wild and raucous revelry.

Yes, Uncle Will was a nasty, mean-tempered man who, although he'd managed to insult and irritate everyone he ever met, had made a sizable fortune bootlegging whiskey during Prohibition. Rotgut whiskey, if I know my Uncle Will.

He died childless. What remained of his estate was divided between my mother and her brothers.

Mom had great plans for her inheritance.

"I bet Uncle Will would spin in his grave if he knew he'd left enough money to make anyone's life easier," Dad said.

"Now, Richard," Mom said. "It ill behooves us to speak disparagingly of the dead."

"Ill behooves" is just the sort of phrase my mother likes to use. She met and married Dad right out of high school and has always felt her education was incomplete. Soon after their marriage Mom announced her plans to read all, and I mean *all*, the Great Books of Literature. She's still going at it tong and hammer.

Mom's the only person I know who has read Dante's *Inferno* instead of the *Soap Opera Digest* under the hair dryer at the Pink Pamper Hair Salon.

My two sisters and I have grown up in the shadow of Mom's lifetime love affair with the pleasures of higher learning, and it's left its mark. Take our names, for example: My twenty-year-old sister Enid was named for a character in Tennyson's poems about King Arthur. My name is Portia because I arrived while Mom was reading *The Merchant of Venice*. And my little sister, Tess, made her appearance twelve years ago smack dab in the middle of *Tess of the D'Urbervilles*.

The morning after Uncle Will's funeral Mom called us all into the den for a family conference. "Your father and I have come to a decision," she announced.

Enid rolled her big periwinkle-blue eyes at me and winked.

It's no secret that all the major decisions in our house are made by Mom. Dad's a jolly, easygoing type who always says, "Yes, Millie dear. I'm sure you know best."

I don't mean to imply that Dad's a pushover or a wimp. He's just totally bewildered by the feminine mystique. Surrounded as he is by three verbal—read that to mean mouthy—and strong-willed daughters, he figures Mom knows how to cope with us better than he does.

Mom cleared her throat importantly. "Your father and I have decided that Uncle Will's legacy should go toward furthering your educations."

Education was the magic word that pushed all Enid's buttons. "Oh, Mother!" she breathed, her face lighting up like the aurora borealis. "How wonderful! How absolutely wonderful!"

My sister is a living legend. Besides being the great beauty of the family, she is also a great brain. For one girl to have everything is grossly unfair, but that's how it is. As Tess once said, "I can really relate to Cinderella's stepsisters when I'm around Enid."

Enid was the youngest graduate in the history of Custisville High School. She left the entire football team, including the water boy, sighing wistfully over how she might have inspired them to greater heights of glory if she had only shelved her books and gone out for Pom-Pom Queen.

Enid was currently attending a local college and was due to graduate in a couple of weeks. Summa cum laude, of course, not to mention Phi Beta Kappa. She'd majored in Elizabethan literature. Her dream was to go on for a master's degree, followed by a Ph.D., and eventually become one of those learned professors who have absolutely the last word in their field.

Maybe I ought to say something here about Tess and me, so you don't get the impression that, by comparison, we're real eyesores who think cat is spelled D-O-G. Neither of us did too badly, either, in the looks department, even though Tess is kind of skinny and has a long way to go before she can even qualify for a training bra. The two of us do bear a faint family resemblance to Enid. We all have the same coloring, sort of, and the same type of features, vaguely. It's just that Tess and I have plain, ordinary old blue eyes while Enid's have been ecstatically described as "twin sapphires." And we're more or less blondish whereas Enid could go on one of those TV hair coloring commercials. You know, where she'd whip her long hair about and say, "I'm expensive, but I'm worth it!"

Do you get the picture?

Tess and I are fairly intelligent, too, but not enough to make our teachers take to the streets yelling, "Eureka!"

Mom, however, insists that we're all brilliant. And that, she says, is because her obstetrician, a forward-looking man, made her inhale a lot of oxygen from a face mask while she was giving birth to us, which activated our brain cells. Or so she claims.

"Now," she stated triumphantly on that Saturday in May, "Dad and I are, at long last, financially able to give you all the educational opportunities you so richly deserve and which, unfortunately, he and I were never privy to."

"Hear! Hear!" cried Dad from his seat in the corner.

Freely translated, in Enid's case, Mom's announcement meant that Enid's graduate school was in the bag. No student loans or waitress jobs for our princess. Uncle Will's ill-gotten gains would make her a professional student until the last syllable of recorded time, or until she got her Ph.D., whichever came first.

Enid tottered off to her room, overcome. As she rounded the bend in the hall, we could hear her mutter, "Yale! Princeton! Harvard! I simply can't believe it!"

"What about me?" Tess asked, looking suspicious.

Tess might have brains, but they're mostly concentrated in her feet. She wants to be a ballerina. A great, famous ballerina, to be more exact. Every night before she turns in she goes through this tedious routine of picking up marbles with her bare toes to strengthen her arches. When she goes en pointe, she says, she wants her "line" to be pure.

"First of all, I'm taking you to the orthodontist to have your overbite corrected," Mom said.

Tess groaned. She thinks her overbite gives her a puckish charm.

"And then," continued Mom, "I'm enrolling you in Countess Nadya Slandowska's School of Russian Ballet."

Tess whooped with joy and bounded straight up from a sitting position. She did a couple of entrechats followed by a flying jeté, knocking over a lamp and sending Archie, the Siamese cat, scurrying for cover.

Until now Tess has been taking ballet lessons at Nellie Swanson's Academy of Dance, a cut-rate school that is to the world of ballet what People's Express was to flying.

"Countess Slandowska's! Wow!" she crowed from midleap. She finally came to rest on one knee, in the traditional ballerina's bow, her arms crossed gracefully over her nonexistent bosom. Hips and boobs, Tess claims, are something no self-respecting danseuse ever cares to possess.

"Countess Slandowska's! Wow!" she repeated. "She's absolutely the tops! But she costs a mint!"

Mom waved her hands. "And worth every penny. When you're dancing your way into the hearts of the crowned heads of Europe, I do hope you remember your Uncle Will with kindness and gratitude."

"Hear! Hear!" said Dad, the turncoat, who has always bad-mouthed Uncle Will.

I wondered what was in store for me.

Actually, I'd been very happy in my freshman year at Custisville High and was looking forward to being a sophomore. My ambitions were modest. I planned to join the staff of the school paper as a roving reporter. I also had a secret hankering to become a pom-pom girl. And, unlike Enid, I was raring to have a go at dating some of the guys on the team. Any team. Football, basketball, baseball, cross-country. The chess team, even. Any team with boys on it. I wasn't fussy.

Mom had that ecstatic look on her face that I know, from long experience, bodes me no good. I had a sinking feeling that what she was going to come up with would improve my mind and my character and make me totally miserable.

"Have you ever heard of Miss Minsham's Academy, Portia?" she asked, the fires of fanaticism burning in her eyes.

"No," I replied with a sinking heart.

"I think you're being deliberately difficult," said Mom. "*Everyone* has heard of Miss Minsham's. It's the finest college preparatory school for girls in the state of Virginia."

I mumbled something.

"What's that? Speak up, dear," Mom said.

"I said I don't want to go to Miss Minsham's, if that's what you're driving at."

"Don't want to go to Miss Minsham's!" Mom placed her hand over her heart to signify deep shock. "Don't want to go to Miss Minsham's! Did you hear that, Richard?"

My father immediately went into an elaborate pantomime of horror and disbelief.

"And why, may I ask," Mom pursued, "wouldn't any normal, intelligent girl *seize* the golden opportunity of going to a fine, private school like that?"

"For one thing, it's all girls."

"Ha!"

"Besides, I like Custisville High just fine."

"I'm not disparaging Custisville High. I simply feel it places an undue importance upon extracurricular activities. *And* boy-girl relationships."

"What's wrong with boy-girl relationships?" I demanded.

"When it comes to frivolous, extracurricular activities and boy-girl relationships, you tend to be flighty and weak. *Weak*, Portia," she repeated with emphasis.

I gave her my best stony stare. Sometimes it works. Sometimes it doesn't. This time it didn't.

"You have a fine mind, Portia," said Mom. "A mind is a terrible thing to waste. I simply won't allow you to do so."

I turned my stony stare into a pout. I even made my lips quiver. That didn't seem to faze Mom, either.

"At the rate you're going, young lady," she continued, warming to the subject, "you're going to wind up a boy-crazy nonachiever."

Achieving is a real biggie to Mom. She's been lecturing us on that subject for as long as I can remember. She's obviously hit the jackpot with Enid the Brain and Tess the Dancing Teenybopper. Two successes out of three wasn't too bad. I didn't know why she wouldn't let me do as I pleased, and I told her just that.

"Why?" she demanded. "Because I love you, that's why. And I want you to realize your full potential. Do you know," she went on, "that the percentage of acceptances from Miss Minsham's to the highest universities in the land is 95.2?"

No, I didn't.

"It even surpasses the acceptance rate of Minsham Academy's brother school, Farnsworth Prep."

"Farnsworth Prep? Brother school?" I snapped out, instantly alert. "Where is it?"

"Just over the hill from Miss Minsham's," Mom said.

"How far over the hill?" I asked.

"Oh, a mile or two," Mom said. "But I don't see what that has to do—"

"How big is it? Farnsworth Prep, I mean."

"It's a large school. Probably about three times the size of Miss Minsham's. But why—"

"So you could say there are approximately three Farnsworth boys to every girl at Miss Minsham's?"

"I guess so, but—"

"Just what, exactly, do you mean by brother school?"

"Well, they get together for things. You know—dances, parties, field meets. Things like that. Properly chaperoned, of course. But—"

"Would I board at Miss Minsham's?"

"Of course. Everyone does. It's out in the country. They have marvelous stables and hiking trails. A sound mind in a healthy body is one of Miss Minsham's stated goals."

"How often would you and Dad come visit?"

"Not very often, I'm afraid," said Mom with a sigh. "Miss Minsham doesn't favor parental intervention."

I gave a silent little cheer for Miss Minsham.

"What makes you think I could qualify? I mean, my grades aren't all that good."

"I've already spoken to Miss Minsham on the phone. Grades, at this point, aren't of paramount importance. She also takes into consideration the results of your IQ tests and your overall ability. Getting you registered should be no problem."

"If I agreed to go, and found out I absolutely loathed it, would you let me quit and come back to Custisville High?"

"Yes, of course, dear. But I'm sure it won't happen."

And that's how I wound up going to Miss Minsham's College Preparatory Academy for Girls.

Chapter Two

Dad said Miss Minsham's Academy was only about three hours from Custisville, as the crow flies. But he must have been following the wrong crow, since it took us nearly four and a half.

Of course, part of our problem was that we got lost umpteen times on some back roads. Mom was supposed to be the navigator, but she has no concept of north and south. The only thing she recognizes on a map is that a big patch of blue signifies a body of water.

I was no help, either. I could barely see out the back window, wedged in as I was amid boxes, suitcases and shoe bags. I was beginning to know how Sweet Betsy from Pike felt as she crossed the wide prairie with her husband Ike.

Now that I'd stopped fighting the idea of attending Miss Minsham's, not that it would do me much good anyway, I was actually looking forward to the school. And the idea of leaving the sometimes-suffocating bosom of my family and being on my own made me feel sophisticated and mature.

All my friends said they were envious of me, which helped. Norma Happlet, whose cousin had gone there, told me it was really a fun school with small classes, great dorm rooms, decent food and lots of social get-togethers with Farnsworth Prep. She told me to be sure and go out for dramatics, because all the male roles in the productions were played by guys from Farnsworth, and rehearsals, during play season, were held *every night*!

I didn't pass any of this information on to my mother. She had some idea the girls at Miss Minsham's were kept as cloistered as medieval nuns, Farnsworth Prep or no. I think she believed that Miss Minsham's motto of A Sound Mind in a Healthy Body signified cold, bracing showers taken daily to mortify our teenage flesh and cool the hot blood of our youth.

Mom's mood, as we drove, alternated between the agony of the coming empty—well, partially empty—nest and the ecstasy of getting her two oldest successfully launched on rich, fulfilling and culturally ennobled lives.

Enid had left the week before for Harvard University. And what a to-do there was getting her ready for departure! Outfitting her with new clothes, luggage and gear for the apartment she'd rented up there was second only in magnitude of preparation to the World War II Allied powers girding up to hit Omaha Beach.

Getting me ready, by comparison, was a lot simpler. But that's how it is when you're the second child. Everything is anticlimactic, somehow.

Enid had taken her Graduate Record Exams earlier in the year and had applied to several of the mossiest and iviest colleges on the Eastern Seaboard, although at the time she hadn't had the foggiest idea how she would meet the cost of tuition. And heaven forbid that our Enid—the name, in Celtic, means *spotless purity*, and Mom sure hit the nail on the head when she named her *that*!—should have to go out into the vulgar marketplace and mingle with the laboring classes to earn her keep.

Anyway, Enid was now safely disposed of, and Tess was spending the weekend with a girl friend, so Mom and Dad could drive me to Miss Minsham's, get me all snuggled down in my dorm and spend Saturday night at the local inn. It was called, appropriately enough, since Minsham's is located deep in the heart of the Virginia hunt country, the Horse and Hounds.

As we drove toward Miss Minsham's, we saw a great many horse farms and huge estates set back from the road. They all had an antebellum look about them— huge, pillared verandas, winding driveways and enclosed paddocks.

There were no photos on any of the many informational brochures Miss Minsham had sent us, but I figured the academy would probably look like something out of *Gone with the Wind* and that probably we'd all be required to get togged out in hoopskirts on Robert E. Lee's birthday and the anniversary of the shelling of Fort Sumter.

A discreet, tastefully lettered sign at the entrance to a small, private road indicated that we had, at last, reached the hallowed grounds of Miss Minsham's Academy.

The road was flanked by a vast area of sloping acreage covered with huge old oak trees whose branches grew close to the ground.

The scene reminded me of Sherwood Forest in that old Robin Hood movie starring Errol Flynn. I expected at any moment to be surrounded by a gaggle of Merrie Men, robbing the rich to give to the poor.

The road inclined upward and, as we rounded the final bend, the paving turned into cobblestones, flanked by a low stone wall on one side.

And there, on the highest point of land, sat the academy. The place was pure Elizabethan Tudor. Enid would have gone bananas over it.

In front of the building was a large cobblestoned courtyard that doubled as a parking lot. Dad parked along the stone wall. We all rolled down our windows, stuck our heads out, and peered up at the academy.

"My goodness!" Mom exclaimed. "This isn't exactly what I pictured."

What we were looking at was the front end of a big E lying on its side. At the center of the building was a large, vaulted entranceway with great oaken double doors and lots of wrought iron—hinges, nail studs, door knockers and big rings where you'd expect to find doorknobs.

"Well, well," said Dad.

"Well, indeed," said Mom.

We got out of the car and walked to the entrance. After having been practically bent double for four and a half hours, I could barely straighten up.

"I hope no one's watching," I said. "They'll think the Hunchback of Notre Dame is checking in."

"Oh, no, they won't," Dad said. "Miss Minsham's doesn't have a football team. Do you get it? Hunchback, fullback! Ha, ha, ha!"

"Control yourself, Richard," said Mom. "We haven't come here to audition for a vaudeville act."

We were greeted at the door by none other than Miss Minsham herself.

She really fitted into the decor. When Mom and Dad took a short trip to England a couple of years ago, they brought back several brass rubbings from old tombs, which Mom promptly had framed at great expense. Miss Minsham was the spitting image of the one of Lady Margaret Plumley, circa 1590. All she needed was a fancy neck ruff, a headdress and a teensy little dog jumping around at her feet to complete the illusion.

Miss Minsham was one of those tall, thin ladies who gets even taller and thinner in their old age. Her gray hair was rolled back in a sort of pompadour all around her head. She wore a longish black dress of no particular era, with white collar and cuffs. A pair of spectacles hung from a black silk cord around her neck. Her face was rather austere-looking, but when she smiled, little laugh crinkles appeared around her eyes, and when we shook hands, her grasp was firm and warm.

"If you'll pull your car around to the rear, Antoine will carry Portia's things up to her room."

She hit a button by the front door and a hollow *bong* reverberated through the halls. Antoine appeared. He was skinny and scraggly with long hair, a beard and a criminal expression on his face. I noticed Mom tuck her purse firmly under her arm, as if she was afraid Antoine would grab it and run.

He really was creepy-looking! What did he do for fun on a Saturday night? I wondered. Pull wings off flies or whip himself with a knotted cord, maybe?

"I'm sure you'd like a tour of the academy," Miss Minsham said pleasantly as Dad went off to move the car, Antoine shambling sinisterly behind him.

"How lovely," Mom said. "But we certainly don't want to take you from your other duties."

"At the moment I have nothing that requires my attention," said Miss Minsham. "You're my first arrivals. Most of the girls will check in tomorrow."

My heart sank, and that is the understatement of all time, as I pictured myself off in a deserted wing, the clocks striking midnight and Antoine on the loose. As a matter of fact, even if they chained him up at night, I wouldn't want to be alone in this big old building. I'd throw myself on Dad and Mom's mercy. They'd have to let me stay with them at the Horse and Hounds.

Miss Minsham cast me an amused glance. She seemed to have the uncanny ability to read the teenage mind.

"You won't be alone, Portia," she said. "A few of the girls will be checking in later this evening. You'll be rooming with three of them who were here last year. They should be a great help in getting oriented."

"Three roommates?" Mom asked.

"Yes. You see, our sophomores are four to a room. Freshmen all share two large communal dormitories on the third floor. Juniors and seniors are semiprivate, with only one other roommate. It works out quite well, spacewise."

"I believe your brochures said you have a student body of under two hundred," Mom said.

"Yes. We try to keep it as small as is economically feasible. When my father and I converted the manor to a boarding school, though, we had to add extra dormitory space to the original wings."

Dad rejoined us at this point, and we set out on what Miss Minsham called an "abbreviated tour."

She wasn't kidding when she said we were the first to arrive. There wasn't another soul to be seen, and because of the high, narrow windows, it was dark inside. I guess Miss Minsham didn't want to run up her lighting bills until everyone got there. The effect was rather eerie.

"My father, who was a banker," Miss Minsham told us, "bought the estate at a distress sale during the Great Depression. He thought it would be a good investment as, indeed, it has been. He got the house and grounds for a song. It had been unoccupied for some time...."

Her voice trailed away. She was evidently remembering something. But what?

I was dying to ask her why it had been unoccupied long enough to sell for a "song." But, for once, I managed to keep my mouth shut.

Then suddenly, unaccountably, I broke out in goose bumps. My grandmother would have said, "A goose is walking over your grave, Portia!" Grandma was Irish and believed in things like little people, ghosts and banshees. I fervently wished I hadn't thought of Grandma and her spook stories my first night away from home.

"The estate was originally named Seaforth's Oaks, after its first owner," Miss Minsham continued, sounding as if she'd given this tour many times. "Robert Seaforth was a down-and-out, newly orphaned English boy of poor parentage who arrived in America in 1870. As it turned out, Mr. Seaforth had a great talent for business and making money. By 1890 he had amassed a large fortune in stocks. Some say his methods weren't quite ethical." A look of contempt passed over Miss Minsham's fine, aristocratic features. "That same year, he built this country estate in the Elizabethan manor house style, sparing no expense. He was compensating, no doubt, for his humble origins. He was quite sensitive about his early poverty, you see. And so—"

"What happened to Mr. Seaforth?" Mom asked abruptly. As I mentioned earlier, she has a real thing about overachievers.

Miss Minsham gave Mom a look that plainly stated that most people never thought to ask that question. "He died. He . . . died. In this house."

"How?" I demanded, forgetting myself. "How did he die?" I always want to hear how people died, so I won't make the same mistake.

Miss Minsham spoke reluctantly. "He...he...was murdered."

"Murdered? *Murdered?*" I cried. Here I was, a newly arrived sophomore who ought to be minding her own business. Nevertheless . . . "Who murdered him? How did it happen? *And in what room?*"

Miss Minsham clearly wanted to terminate this unpleasant dialogue. She spoke hurriedly and, I thought, evasively.

"He was murdered by a mad French maid who subsequently committed suicide. It was quite tragic. But that was a long time ago and we won't dwell on it, will we, dear? Come, let me show you the rooms on this floor."

I was simply dying to find out more about that mad French maid. Did she commit suicide here, at the academy? Would I be spending what were supposed to be the best years of my life on the site of a gory murder-suicide? Just what had Mom gotten me into now?

On the other hand, Norma Happlet had said it was a "fun" school. So maybe Miss Minsham was right. Whatever happened was over and done with long, long ago. I felt a little more cheerful.

To the left of the foyer where we now stood was an area partitioned off into several school offices and a small infirmary. Miss Minsham told us it had once been an enormous formal drawing room. The wing that adjoined it on this floor, she said, was used for classrooms.

To the right of the foyer was a reception room, beautifully paneled in a dark, antiqued oak, with several sofas and a number of easy chairs and tables. Over the marble fireplace hung an oil portrait of Good Queen Bess.

"We don't normally allow any students in here," Miss Minsham explained. "It's used only by visitors and members of the staff."

Directly in front of the foyer was the old ballroom, now used as an auditorium. A stage had been built at its far end. On the left wall was what I would call a walk-in fireplace, large enough to roast an ox in, if you had a craving for roast ox, that is. On the same wall, beyond the fireplace, open windows on the second floor looked down on the ballroom.

"In Elizabethan times this would have been the minstrels' gallery," Miss Minsham said, pointing upward. "Mr. Seaforth was quite faithful in reproducing the traditional manor house of that era."

Then she led us through the ballroom and out a door into what was called the Great Hall and which had once been a long portrait gallery. I wondered whose portraits Mr. Seaforth had hung there. An impressive flight of broad pink marble stairs led up to the second floor.

We continued on down the Great Hall, turned a corner and entered the library. It must always have been a library, I noted. There were floor-to-ceiling bookshelves on all sides done in the same dark paneled oak we'd seen everywhere. A pair of French doors led out to a beautifully landscaped garden.

"As you can see," Miss Minsham said, "this is quite a large old building and you've seen just a small portion of it. Unfortunately I've shown you as much as time allows today. Perhaps on your next visit Portia can give you a tour of the rest."

She pressed another button in the library. Again a *bong* resounded through the building. "I'll have one of the staff take Portia to her dormitory room and help her unpack. We won't be serving dinner tonight, but I'm sure you would like to dine together. The food at the Horse and Hounds is superb."

I was positively feverish with fright that Antoine would come to escort me to my room. However, a pleasant-faced young woman named Violet, wearing a white uniform, appeared.

Mom and Dad said they'd be back in an hour to pick me up for an early dinner.

As I followed Violet through the dimly lit corridors and up several flights of winding stairs to the sophomore dorm, I kept asking myself: Where was he murdered? The ballroom? The library? The reception room? And with what? Dagger? Pistol? Fire tongs?

Enid always complains that I have a wild, undisciplined imagination. Maybe that was why I was beginning to think I was the heroine of a Gothic novel.

Chapter Three

My room was surprisingly cheery.

I felt like Snow White just after she'd blundered into the Seven Dwarfs' sleeping quarters.

Along one side of the wall, lined up neatly, were four single beds, all with matching green-and-white bedspreads. A maple nightstand was at the head of each, with a student's desk and chair at each foot. I hope Miss Minsham isn't big on homework, I thought, looking at the desks.

I picked the bed farthest away from the door. If Antoine got some dark compulsion to wander during the full moon, he'd have to murder three others before he got to me.

Violet helped me unpack and stow away my belongings in the wardrobe and bureau. She said she would have someone take my suitcases to the storage room and dispose of the empty boxes.

"Does everyone get all this help?" I asked her. "I feel like I've just checked into the New York Hilton."

"Only the newcomers," Violet answered. "After you've been here awhile, you're treated just like family, honey."

When the last suitcase had been unpacked, it was nearly time to meet Dad and Mom. Violet pointed out a few navigational landmarks on our return pilgrimage to the front foyer. She insisted that in no time at all I'd know every nook and cranny in the building.

"Now *that*," I said, quoting my mother, "is a consummation devoutly to be wished!"

"Huh?" said Violet.

The dinner at the Horse and Hounds was probably the most depressing meal of my entire life. We were sitting in a little booth made to resemble a horse's stall, except that the enclosure was only shoulder high. Mom kept saying how *wonderful* it was that I was going to a *wonderful* boarding school like *wonderful* Miss Minsham's, and then she'd start weeping into a big wad of Kleenex she'd dredged up from her carryall.

To tell you the truth, I was feeling pretty teary myself. It's painful to both parties, you know, when you cut the old umbilical cord. At that point I wasn't being very sophisticated or mature.

"For Pete's sake, Millie," Dad said, "you're attracting attention."

"So let them look," Mom sniffed. "I'm a mother. I'm entitled."

"Listen, Mom," I said, "if you want, I'll come back to Custisville with you. Tonight!"

"Over my dead body," said Mom.

This scene replayed itself many times during dinner, and by the time the waiter brought our check, the family at the next table was staring at us as if we were a made-for-TV special movie presentation.

I couldn't help staring back. They were probably the best-looking family trio I'd ever seen. To look at them nearly made my eyes water.

The father was tall and robust with a shock of prematurely gray hair framing his ruddy face. The mother was completely different, and as exotically beautiful as her husband was handsome. Her eyes were as black as onyx, and her thick dark hair was pulled straight back from her perfect features into a sort of figure-eight-type bun.

The daughter had the kind of looks I would die for. Her hair was thick and glossy and perfectly straight. It was dark, like her mother's, and she wore it parted in the middle and hanging down around her shoulders with just the barest hint of an underturned page-boy at the ends.

Her skin was creamy, and she looked as if she'd probably never had a zit in her life. To top it off, she had the kind of cheekbones that movie starlets pay makeup artists a fortune to reproduce with blusher and highlighter.

Her mouth was small and beautifully shaped with perfect teeth, naturally! The most arresting feature in all this impossible pulchritude, though, were her eyes. They were large and tilted slightly up at the outer corners, under heavy lashes and dark wings of perfectly pruned eyebrows. And even in the semigloom of the Horse and Hounds, I could see that they were green. No, not green. Emerald. She looked to be about my age. I wondered if we'd be classmates at Miss Min-sham's.

And then she burst the bubble.

She stared hard at me with a kind of mean expression on her face, then turned and said something to her mother in a sly undertone. Her mother made a gesture, as though chiding her daughter for being rude. It didn't seem to faze Miss American Beauty, though. She just turned her green gaze on me again and sniggered.

Yes, sniggered. It destroyed the whole illusion. Suddenly, before my very eyes, the Queen of the May turned into Lady Macbeth, Junior.

"Please Lord," I prayed, "don't let her be one of my roommates!"

I didn't have much time to expand on my prayer, since the waiter was back in a trice with our change. Dad tipped him handsomely in spite of Mom's remonstrances, and then we were out in the parking lot, into the car and headed back to the academy.

I won't go into the heavy parting scene at the front entrance. It was pretty painful. Dad even blubbered a little, then pulled himself together and said, "Now, Millie, we'll be back in just a couple of weeks for Parents Weekend."

The halls were still dimly shrouded in light as I made my way back to the sophomore dorm, which made me grateful to Violet for her routing directions. I was able to find my way up the back stairs and down the hall to my room without getting lost more than once or twice.

I'd planned to take a quick shower and then hop into bed where I could shed a few more tears for my lost childhood before my roommates arrived. But that wasn't to be the case. As I drew nearer, I saw that the door to my room was ajar. Lights were blazing and I heard a lot of chattering and giggling and, now and then, a loud hoot of laughter.

Great! I thought, mopping my damp cheeks hurriedly with a soggy tissue. Hail, hail, the gang's all here. I shoved the door open, pasted a cheerful smile on my face and prepared to meet my new roommates.

Chapter Four

They all looked up when I entered.

Two girls were sitting cross-legged on one of the beds. The third, a dark-haired girl who looked like a teen version of Sophia Loren, reclined on the floor alongside. A big Care package of cookies and fudge was scattered in their midst.

"Hi!" I chirped as heartily as I could under the circumstances. "I guess you're my roommates. I'm Portia. Portia Johnson."

There was dead silence for the space of several heartbeats while they sized me up. I guess I passed inspection. The brunette on the floor stood up and came over to me with a friendly smile.

"Hi, Portia. I'm Dee Campo. We thought you'd *never* get here. I've been trying to save you some of the fudge, but Marylou here is making a total pig of herself. She's a chocaholic, poor thing!"

One of the girls on the bed, a slender redhead with a heart-shaped face and big brown eyes, smiled sheepishly and pointed to her T-shirt. On it was printed: In Case of Emergency, Please Administer Chocolate. I gathered this was Marylou.

"And I'm Pam," said the third in a musical voice. "But, Dee," she said, "let's do these introductions properly. You have absolutely no couth."

Pam turned back to me. I liked her immediately. She had a pleasant face—mischievous-looking blue eyes, a ski-jump nose and pink, pink cheeks. Long wavy brown hair kept falling forward over her face. Every now and then she'd flip it back impatiently and tuck it behind her ears.

"I'm Pam Shultz, and don't you dare call me Shultzy," she said. "Only my enemies call me Shultzy. And Marylou's last name is Maloney. She'd have to have a name like Maloney with that red hair, wouldn't she? Oh, and watch out for her temper. She's a real wild woman."

"I am not a wild woman," Marylou protested. "I'm really a very nice person."

Dee laughed. "Pam's just teasing, Portia. She has a weird sense of humor. Actually, Marylou is our resident saint. I've never seen her get mad at anyone. Not even at Raquel Finnerty. Raquel, by the way, is our resident pain in the neck."

"*Neck* is the wrong anatomical part," said Pam.

I hung my jacket in my wardrobe and joined them, perching on an adjoining bed. "There's so much I need to know about Miss Minsham's," I said. "First of all, what are the classes like? I've been worried about that. Are they hard?"

"Some are, some aren't," said Dee, shrugging her shoulders.

"They're all easy for you, Dee," sighed Marylou. "I'm the one who always has trouble. I'm so glad I have smart roomies."

"We'll get our schedules Monday and talk to our counselor. Gosh, I hope I'm down for biology," said Pam, helping herself to another chocolate chip cookie. Belatedly she remembered her manners and passed the box to me.

"Why? Are you interested in science?" I asked. "Personally the thought of cutting up a chloroformed frog makes my blood run cold."

Pam closed her eyes and swayed dreamily. "If your blood runs cold in biology as taught here at Miss Minsham's, you need hormone injections. Mr. Hamilton, the science teacher, is a living doll. When he turns those Mel Gibson eyes on you, you'll be willing to cut up anything—your grandmother, even!"

"There she goes again," complained Dee. "Pam's a fool for love, and that's a fact."

Pam opened her eyes. "Me? A fool for love? Marylou is the one who's always in love. Ask her, Portia, who had three dates to the Spring Formal at Farnsworth Prep."

Marylou blushed furiously. "That wasn't love. I was just being polite. I didn't know how to turn anybody down without hurting his feelings."

"You went to the dance with *three* dates?" I asked incredulously.

"No. She palmed the extra ones off on Pam and me," said Dee. "I got Harvey Snelling. That poor boy had such a crush on Marylou that we wound up following her around the dance floor every time they played a slow one. I danced backward half the night.''

"And I got Ed of the Eighteen Arms," Pam said. "Ugh!"

"Ed of the Eighteen Arms?" I asked.

Marylou looked exasperated. "I don't know why you have to call Ed Hogan by that awful name, Pam. He's a very nice boy. A nice, shy boy."

"Maybe with you he's shy. With me he's a passion-crazed beast! *You* he wants to take home to meet his mother. *Me* he wants to drag behind a bush to meet my fate. A fate worse than death!" Pam threw herself dramatically on the bed.

Dee looked at me, sighed resignedly and shook her head. Obviously there was no stopping Pam when she'd sunk her teeth into a dramatic role.

"Maybe it's just me!" Pam emoted. "Oh, what have I got? Why can't they leave me alone? Oh, the curse of being a sex object!"

One thing's for sure, I thought. I'm not going to be bored around these three.

"Since when are *you* a sex object, Shultzy?" cooed a snide voice from the open doorway. "Maybe you're just fantasizing, huh?"

Pam sat up abruptly. "Remember what I said about the name Shultzy, Portia? I mean, about the type of people who call me Shultzy? Hello-o-o-o-o, Raquel," she said to the girl in the doorway. "Please don't feel you have to apologize for interrupting an extremely private conversation. And I hope you're not embarrassed about eavesdropping."

My jaw fell open. The new arrival was none other than the girl I'd seen at the Horse and Hounds.

Raquel turned her emerald eyes on me. "I know you. You sat at the next table when I was having dinner with Mother and Father."

Maybe she won't bring up the fact that Mom had cried and blown her nose through the entire meal, I hoped. I was wrong.

"Your mother was *so-o-o* funny," Raquel said, "the way she bawled and carried on. I guess she just hated to part with her dear little baby girl."

"Well, now, isn't that strange," I retorted. "Your mother looked positively joyful. You'd almost think she was celebrating something. Getting rid of you, maybe?"

Raquel didn't say anything. She just glared at me and left the room.

"That was beautiful, Portia!" crowed Dee.

"Oh boy," I said glumly, "I've only been here a few hours and I've made an enemy already."

"It doesn't take long with our dear Raquel," said Pam.

"What's the matter with her? Why is she like that?" I asked. "She's so pretty. She could have everything going for her if she wanted. What's her problem?"

"She's just spoiled," said Marylou.

"Spoiled rotten," put in Pam. "She's a rotten, spoiled little b—"

"Raquel's the only child of immensely wealthy parents," Dee interrupted hastily. "They simply dote on her and cater to her every whim and fancy. Her mother's family is very upper class. Evidently they were once Spanish aristocrats who owned half of California before it became a state. They owned half of Texas, too. Somebody told me one of her ancestors fought at the battle of the Alamo, on the Mexican side, of course. He didn't want to lose his couple million acres to the Yankees.''

"I bet he was the one who shot Davey Crockett," Pam muttered darkly.

"Does she have any friends?" I asked.

"Not friends, exactly," Dee said. "Sycophants."

"Huh?" said Marylou.

"A sycophant is a servile flatterer, Marylou," explained Dee.

"Well," Marylou said, "I don't think we ought to be talking about Raquel Finnerty and her sy-sy... er, servile flatterers. We don't want to give Portia a bad impression her very first night here at the academy. Let's talk about something nice."

"What I want to hear about is the murder-suicide," I said.

"What murder-suicide?" asked Marylou, looking blank.

"You know. The mad French maid and all that," I said.

Marylou blinked her brown eyes in bewilderment. "Mad French maid? Do you mean Violet? Violet isn't French. And the only time I've ever seen her get mad was when we all had a big soap fight last year and messed up the showers."

"I think Portia is referring to the story about Mr. Seaforth's murder by the mad—mad meaning insane, Marylou dear—French maid who supposedly killed herself afterward," said Dee.

"I certainly don't know anything about that!" said Marylou.

"I'm dying, if you'll pardon the expression, to hear all about it," I said.

"I don't know much," Dee said doubtfully. "No one seems to. All the details, I mean. Miss Minsham doesn't like anyone to talk about it. Bad for the school image and all that."

"Some of the senior girls told us a little about it last year, during freshman initiation," said Pam. "They wanted to scare us, so I don't know how much of what they said was true."

"What, exactly, did they say?" I asked.

"Let me see," said Pam. "I'll try to remember. Actually, those senior girls scared me more than any mad murderer would. Remember that big one, Dee, with the hairy legs? The one who said she'd hang me out the window if I kept shooting my mouth off?"

"The murder, Pam," I reminded her. "What about the murder?"

"Well, they said Mr. Seaforth was a real rat. A crook and a rat. He made a lot of money in shady business deals. He was a real fink."

"Yes! Yes! Please go on!"

"Well, our dear old Mr. Seaforth was a rat in more ways than one. He also played it fast and loose with the ladies, if you know what I mean. I'm surprised he isn't hanging around the dorm haunting me. I seem to attract that type."

"You've gone into all that before, Pam. Please, just stick to the facts."

"All right. It seems Mr. Seaforth had a real thing going with one of the maids. A young Frenchwoman. She thought he was a man of honor and that he would marry her. Ha! Fat chance! He wasn't about to hook up with a servant. He was looking for a rich, blue-blooded debutante."

"Did he find one?"

"Oh, yes. A daughter of one of the local gentry. And the French maid was totally devastated. The morning after he announced his engagement to this heiress, whoever she was, the maid caught him alone and blasted him off to kingdom come with a pistol. Then she killed herself. That's all I know."

"I don't remember all that," Dee marveled.

"It sort of imprinted itself on my memory as I was hanging upside down by my feet from a window," said Pam.

"Isn't there something about a ghost?" prompted Dee.

"Oh, yes. That's the fun part," said Pam. "Those seniors told us that the mad French maid haunts the school."

"I don't remember any of this," Marylou said. "And I've certainly never seen any ghost."

"I don't think anyone has," said Pam. "Those rotten seniors were probably just putting us on. I don't even know if they had the facts straight."

"Where did the murder-suicide take place?" I wanted to know.

"They didn't say. It had to be in one of the original old rooms, though. But, as I said, no one knows the exact, true story."

"Well, where there's smoke there's fire, as my mother always says," I remarked.

"Hey! Your mother has some real original sayings," said Pam. "Tell us more."

By the time we turned out the lights and crawled into our narrow little beds, I'd told the others all about my family, and Great-Uncle Will, and how it happened I'd wound up at the academy.

Dee told me her parents had died when she was a baby, and that her Aunt Edna had raised her.

"Aunt Edna is sweet, but she says she simply can't begin to cope with the problems of a teenager. That's why I'm here."

Marylou said her mother was a TV actress and was currently playing the role of Lila Lamour in the long-running soap opera *Kiss Tomorrow Goodbye* and that she'd just divorced her fourth husband.

"Mama says it isn't good for me to be around all that show biz glitz. She says Miss Minsham's can give me a nice, stable environment. She's right. It is kind of confusing to keep getting new stepfathers all the time. I don't know why she gets rid of them. They were all very nice."

"Have you noticed, Portia, that 'nice' is Marylou's favorite adjective? She thinks everybody's nice," said Dee.

"Well, I do," Marylou insisted. "They are!"

"With a few notable exceptions," put in Pam. "Like Adolf Hitler, Attila the Hun and Raquel Finnerty. You know, Portia, I once bet Marylou she couldn't go all day without saying nice."

"Who won?"

"Guess," said Pam. "It was the easiest dollar I ever earned."

At that point, Dee and Marylou declared they needed their sleep and would we please just hush up. Hush up was how Marylou put it. Shut up was Dee's.

Pam, however, kept chattering on.

"I'm here because they have a great music department. I've been taking voice lessons since I was knee-high to a nightingale. My vocal cords ought to be insured by Lloyds of London. What I want to do is be a big star on Broadway and meet some old millionaire who will shower me with jewels and furs."

"I'm going to shower you with rocks in another minute," Dee grumbled sleepily.

Pam was quiet for a few minutes. Then she began to moan. "OOOOOOH! I ate too many cookies. I think I'm going to puke!"

"How many times do I have to tell you, Pam," Marylou said. "The word is vomit, not puke!"

"Regurgitate is more genteel," put in Dee.

"Well, if it's going to start an argument, I've changed my mind," Pam said. "I'm not going to puke after all."

I was still smiling when I fell asleep.

Chapter Five

Back in the forties and fifties, Hollywood made a lot of movies where the passing of time was shown by the fluttering of a bunch of calendar pages. That's what my first week at Miss Minsham's was like.

I was so busy with new classes, making friends and getting adjusted to, as Mom would say, the Boarding School Experience, not to mention spending hours in giggling sessions with Pam, Dee and Marylou, that I didn't have time to be homesick.

To tell the truth, and I'm ashamed to admit this, I hadn't even thought much about my family at all. So, at Friday's mail call, when I was handed a bulky letter from Mom, I felt a sharp stab of guilt. Here I was up to my hips in a new adventure and loving every minute of it while my poor abandoned parents were probably crying themselves to sleep every night.

Mom wrote:

My dear, brave darling,

When your father and I set out for home, needless to say, I could scarcely see the road for the scalding tears that bedimmed my eyes.

I kept asking Dad if we had done the right thing, leaving you, as we had, to an uncertain fate in a nest of strangers. More than once I wondered aloud if we should turn back. Dad buoyed my flagging spirits, however, by relating several amusing anecdotes concerning the first time he went away to Boy Scout camp.

And that reminds me, do they indulge in the practice of short-sheeting beds at Miss Minsham's? If so, I do hope you'll tell them, and *forcefully*, Portia, *not* to do it. You need your sleep. As Shakespeare says, "Sleep knits the raveled sleeve of care." And I'm sure your cares are many, being on your own as you are.

If you want to come home, Portia dear, tell us so. *Immediately!!!* And don't worry if your decision brings on one of my crippling attacks of vertigo for which there is *no known medical cure*! I am your mother, Portia. I only want what's best for you, no matter what price *I* must pay. After all, wasn't I willing to walk through the Valley of the Shadow in giving you birth?

By the way, darling, if you're *not* coming home, I hope you won't mind if I turn your room into an artist's studio. Naturally I won't remove any of your furniture, but will merely bring in my easel, paints, canvases, drop cloths, etc.

Yes! Artist's studio! I signed up for an art class at the Community Center. Palette knife techniques. We had our first class yesterday and, if I may say so, I show great promise.

Our instructor wanted us to start off by painting an apple or orange or something piddling like that. When I told her my first endeavor would be to copy Van Gogh's *Starry Night*, she was quite speechless with admiration. It's coming along nicely, except for the spots where the cat rubbed up against it.

Oh, I nearly forgot! Enid will be home for your school's Parents Weekend. Both she and Tess will accompany us when we visit you.

Enid loves graduate school and will tell you all about it when she sees you. Tess complains about the braces on her teeth but, as I tell her, There Are No Gains Without Pains. One cannot have an Easter Sunday without a Good Friday. Fortune Favors the Bold! Keep those uplifting thoughts in mind, Portia.

I miss you terribly, dearest. *Terribly!*

> *A Bientôt,*
> Mother

PS: Now that I'm an artist I *must* start thinking in French!

Somehow, I'm not quite sure how, my mother's letter cheered me up considerably and relieved my sense of guilt. I did make a mental note, though, to write a long letter home that very night.

I liked my classes. Well, most of them.

Along with the usual sophomore courses, I was also taking Latin II and biology. Mom always insisted I take four years of Latin so that I could read the clas-

sics in the original. This year we'd be doing Caesar.
We'd just learned that Gaul was divided into three
parts, and I wasn't particularly interested in any of
them. With luck, maybe, I could switch to Spanish in
my junior year. It's easier than Latin and a lot more
romantic.

And speaking of romantic, Mr. Hamilton, the
biology teacher, was everything Pam had described.
He did look like Mel Gibson. And, oh, those blue,
blue eyes! When he got up in front of his little black-
board, no head nodded. Every eye was positively riv-
eted on his manly face and form.

I figured he probably lifted weights in his spare
time. No one could have a body like that without outside help. And, to make him even more interesting, as
if that was necessary, Mr. Hamilton was a bonafide
bachelor.

Pam sat next to me in class, so I had to listen to her
rapturous moanings and speculations on Mr. Hamilton's love life. She was my lab partner, too, which was
handy, because she said she'd do all the dissecting if
I'd type up the notes.

When we got our class schedules, I wasn't sure what
activity I'd pick for PE.

"For Pete's sake," Pam warned. "Don't go out for
field hockey."

"Why?" I asked, not that I had any burning desire
to play field hockey.

"Because that's Raquel Finnerty's forte! With her
criminal instincts, she just loves to get out there with
her trusty little hockey stick and legally bash, cripple
and maim. The way you two have been mixing it up,
she'd have your teeth on a platter the very first day!"

I hadn't exactly been "mixing it up" with Raquel, but we'd had a few face-offs. Raquel was rooming with three of her sycophants, as Dee called them. One was a girl named Jane. Jane was tall and anorexic-looking, with hipbones that jutted a mile out of all her skirts, even the ones with pleats and gathers. Jane said she was going to be a high-fashion model, and from the grim expression she always wore on her face, I figured she was probably consuming a pound or more a day of laxatives to keep thin.

The other two roommates were a couple of look-alike nonentities whom Raquel kept about her strictly for their muscle power. Their names were Sybil and Regan. Sybil was moon-faced and nasty. Regan—the name of one of King Lear's daughters, one of the murderous ones, I recall—was just plain nasty.

I had to admit, when those four came down the hall toward you, en masse, it made the bowels of the timid turn to water from sheer fright.

My first confrontation with Raquel was on Sunday, the day after I'd checked into Miss Minsham's. Ever since I can remember, every night I've prayed for the strength and intelligence to keep my big mouth shut. So far my prayers haven't been answered.

Actually, it was all Raquel's fault. She and her terrible threesome had cornered a group of arrivals—new girls, like myself—and were lecturing them on the quality and superiority of her wardrobe.

"Every one of my sweaters," I heard her say, "is cashmere. Pure, one hundred percent cashmere. Man-made yarns are so tacky, don't you agree?"

One poor girl, a shy, nervous type named Jennifer, who looked as if she needed someone to protect her, was actually shrinking back and crossing her arms to hide her acrylic pullover. So guess who had to rush in to defend her and the American Way of Life?

I said, "I'm surprised you have such a scientific interest in clothing fibers, Raquel. I mean, considering the fact that the skirt you're wearing is definitely rump-sprung and the warp and woof look like they're under terrible stress. Have you, maybe, put on a little weight lately?"

Living with Mom and her literary turn of phrase has given me a real Clarence Darrow way of speaking when I'm being snotty, as you may have noticed.

There were a few more incidents.

One was when Raquel and her buddies were following a chubby girl named Melba down the hall. Raquel was amusing her friends by doing an imitation of Melba's walk. She was waddling and flapping her arms and making duck sounds. I knew Melba knew what was going on behind her because her ears were a brilliant pink.

The caped crusader swooped to the rescue again.

"Raquel, dear," I said, heaving to alongside, "you do a terrible imitation of a duck. You really ought to try doing a horse's rear end. It's more up your alley, somehow."

And when Raquel was going on about her wealthy and distinguished Spanish grandee ancestors in the dining hall, I just had to say: "Isn't it wonderful that our country is such a melting pot of cultures. But how sad that so many of them produced nothing but nerds and duds in their descendants."

There was a small scattering of applause at that one, along with a few muffled cheers.

Dee told me later that I was fast getting the reputation among the younger girls for being a modern-day female Zorro, dashing in to rescue the oppressed and all that.

Anyway, in the short span of a few days, I had definitely become number one on the Raquel Finnerty hit list.

"Portia, why do you keep baiting Raquel?" Marylou asked. "She can be really ugly when she's crossed."

"I admire what you're doing, Portia," Dee said, "but aren't you coming on a bit strong?"

"Keep up the good work, Portia," Pam said. "You're the first girl at Miss Minsham's with the guts to tell off Raquel and her henchpersons! *Viva la revolución!*"

The feud with Raquel Finnerty was definitely on!

Chapter Six

A mixer, in case you've never been to one, is just your basic Saturday night high school dance, except, in this case, those attending were from different schools. The idea is that everyone is supposed to mix and mingle and chat it up so that by the end the group is one big happy family.

My roommates told me this wasn't exactly what always happened.

"Sometimes you get stuck right from the start with a boy you don't particularly like, and you don't get a chance to meet anyone else," Dee complained.

"I never know how to get rid of somebody, once I've danced with him," Marylou said. "It seems so rude just to say thank-you and walk away. I mean, what if he has an inferiority complex or something?"

"I wouldn't want to walk away from any of the ones you attract, Marylou," said Pam. "You always get the cute, interesting ones."

Marylou was a member of the social committee, so she was able to give us the boy-girl statistics on the dance. "All the freshman and sophomore girls are coming," she told us. "Only a few juniors are turning out for it, and we don't have a single senior on our list. They say they've mixed with Farnsworth enough to last them the rest of their lives. They're all out looking for college men this year."

"Goody-goody," Pam said. "All the more for us!"

"How many boys from Farnsworth are coming?" I said. "Is there a good boy-girl ratio?"

Marylou flipped open her stenographic pad and studied her notes. "Let's see. Hmm. Yes, here it is. We have 2.5 boys for every girl. The committee is really pleased with the turnout."

"I sure hope I don't get that half a guy," said Pam. "I've danced with some real oddballs in my time, but never with someone who's only half-human. On second thought, maybe I have."

"But how many of the Farnsworth boys are freshmen?" I persisted. "We're only interested in the older ones."

Marylou consulted her notes again. "It looks like the entire freshman class is coming."

"Oh, burp, yuck!" said Pam.

"And most of the sophomores. A lot of juniors, too. But we aren't sure about the seniors."

"Why not?" I asked.

"Because the senior sign-up sheet was filled with names like George Washington and Will Shakespeare and Jack D. Ripper."

"Smart alecks!" snorted Pam.

"The older girls on the committee, though," Marylou continued, "say we'll probably get a number of seniors. There are always some who are out looking for younger girls."

"Marvelous," said Pam. "We're getting all the kinky ones."

For all her bad-mouthing of the Farnsworth boys, Pam took great pains with her appearance that night. She decked herself out in a frilly lace blouse and a taffeta skirt. Ruffles don't exactly suit Pam's personality, but I wasn't about to be the one to point that out to her.

"And look at my shoes," she said, sticking her foot out and admiring it. "Three-inch heels with ankle straps. I'll probably break my neck in them, but they do make my legs look sort of sexy, don't they?"

Marylou, in a beautifully cut green dress with a white Peter Pan collar, her red hair brushed until it shone like a newly minted penny, looked like something out of a storybook.

Dee, quiet, studious Dee, was absolutely stunning in a deep burgundy wraparound. The color made her olive skin glow and set off her big brown eyes. The tightly belted sash showed her movie star figure to perfection.

Pam squinted at her appraisingly. "You didn't look this good last year, Dee. What have you done to yourself?"

"It's called maturation, Pam," replied Dee. "I had nothing to do with it."

"Well, don't stand next to me in the wallflower lineup. You make me look like a skinny, underfed, ten-year-old boy."

My yellow dress was buttoned down the front and had a wide belt and a slim skirt. The color did a lot for my complexion. I felt pretty satisfied with myself.

"I must say," Dee commented, "we are an unusually good-looking foursome. The world is ours tonight."

"Take *no* prisoners!" said Pam.

I went downstairs ahead of the rest. Miss Sturgeon, our English Lit teacher and head chaperon for the evening—Pam called her the Virgin Sturgeon—had asked me to help out with the setting-up.

When I reached the foyer, Miss Sturgeon was dashing around, looking distraught and wringing her hands.

"I'm glad you're here, Portia. There's so much to do and the committee is occupied elsewhere. Would you please pop into the reception room and turn on the lights? *All* the lights. We don't want any couples sneaking off into dimly lit rooms and getting into...er...compromising situations. And while you're at it, plump up the pillows on the sofas and open a few windows."

"Yes, Miss Sturgeon," I replied dutifully.

When I opened the door to the reception room, I was hit with a blast of cold air, although the day had been unseasonably warm. It was dark as pitch in there, and it took a few minutes of fumbling to find the light switch.

And then it happened.

As I was turning on the lights, I had the eerie sensation that there was someone, or something, in the room with me.

Have you ever heard the expression, "My hair stood on end"? Well, it's true.

The lights revealed an empty room, but the hairs on the nape of my neck thought otherwise. They positively shot straight out from my scalp. There was something creepy in there, and I didn't wait to find out what it was.

I barreled out of the room at top speed and nearly collided with Pam, who was mincing along the hall in her new high heels.

"Thank heaven you're here, Pam," I babbled. "I was just in the reception room, and I swear my hair is standing on end!"

Pam looked at me critically. "There's nothing wrong with your hair. You look just fine. My goodness, you're a bag of nerves tonight. Haven't you ever been to a dance before?"

"Listen to me, Pam," I said, grabbing her by her frilly lapels. "There's something—"

"Let go of me, you maniac!" Pam squeaked. "You're mashing my blouse!"

"That reception room! There's something—"

"Now you did it!" gasped Pam, wrenching herself from my fevered clutches. "You popped one of my bra straps!"

"But, Pam—"

"And it was the last clean bra in my drawer!"

"Listen to me, Pam. Listen to me. I'm trying to tell you something. It was so spooky—"

"You're darn right I look spooky," snapped Pam. "Thanks to you, I look like some sort of lopsided mutant. If I can't find a safety pin, Portia, you're dead meat. Good Lord, can't you control your anxiety attacks?"

Pam went off, muttering under her breath and shooting me dirty looks over her shoulder.

I pressed my forehead against the cool wood of the foyer archway and took a few deep breaths. That's where I was when Dee found me.

"I've just had the most awful experience," I told her.

Dee led me into the empty auditorium and sat me down on one of the side chairs. Miss Sturgeon and the social committee were nowhere in sight. They were probably down in the basement bringing up the punch and cookies.

"What happened, Portia? You look like you've just seen a ghost."

"I think maybe I have."

"Try to calm yourself and tell me exactly what happened."

"I'm not too sure, Dee. I went into the reception room to turn on the lights and ... and ..."

"And?"

"I don't know. There was something creepy in there."

"Maybe you're just overexcited, this being your first dance with Farnsworth Prep and all."

"I am *not* overexcited. Do you really think I'm overexcited about a silly dance?"

"Did you see anything in the reception room?"

"No, I didn't see anything," I replied testily. "That's the point I'm trying to make. It wasn't what I *saw*, it's what I *felt*!"

Dee sighed. "Look, Portia, you seem to have some kind of fixation on that old ghost of the mad French maid story. Let's rationalize your fears. No one has ever seen a ghost in there, as far as I know."

"A lot you know!"

"It's probably just a legend. Now, we all know you're sensitive and imaginative...."

"I am not!" I snapped.

"And you went into the room, in the dark, in a slightly overwrought state...."

"I'm not overwrought! I'm not overwrought! I'm not overwrought!" I shrieked.

"And you thought you felt a supernatural presence," said Dee.

I tried a new attack. Trying to sound sane and sensible, I said, "Look, Dee, is there any chance that the mad French maid shot Mr. Seaforth in the reception room and committed suicide there?"

"That's always a possibility, but—"

"And that's why no one has ever actually seen the ghost, since students are rarely allowed in there."

"Maybe, but—"

The auditorium had begun to fill with chattering females. Miss Sturgeon had reappeared and was shouting excited commands that nobody was obeying. Marylou was testing the stereo equipment. I could hear her voice on the loudspeaker saying, "Am I plugged in?" *Squeeeeeeeek.* "Can you hear me?"

I looked Dee in the eye and said as slowly and as intelligently as possible, "Dee, there is *something* in that reception room, and I'm going to get to the bottom of it."

Dee's mouth was moving, saying something, but I couldn't hear her because, at that point, the front door was flung open and the boys from Farnsworth Prep came swarming in.

I forgot all about the ghost of the mad French maid. I forgot what day or year it was. I almost forgot my own name.

For there, spearheading the right front flank, was the boy I'd been dreaming about all my life. Well, since I hit puberty, anyway.

He looked at me. I looked at him. Two strangers across a crowded room.

And then, in my imagination, the strains of the overture to Tchaikovsky's *Romeo and Juliet* swelled and filled the haunted halls of Miss Minsham's Academy for Girls.

Chapter Seven

He said his name was Hugo Miller.

Hugo?

Yes, I know Hugo isn't a romantic name, especially for someone who looks more like a Raoul or a Leonardo. Tall, dark, handsome. Flashing eyes. Crooked smile, but straight teeth. A boy like Hugo Miller, though, could cast a romantic allure over a name like Mortimer Snerd, even.

As he took my arm and led me onto the dance floor, I was thinking, Mr. and Mrs. Hugo Miller. Mrs. Hugo Miller. Portia Johnson Miller. Hugo and Portia. Portia and Hugo. Ms. Portia Miller. Whither you go, I go, Hugo.

"But everyone calls me Hugh," my dreamboat was saying. "I really hate the name Hugo. I don't know what ever made my mother decide to call me that."

I mentally scrapped the "Mrs. Hugo Miller" in favor of "Mrs. Hugh Miller." It had a nicer ring to it.

The music started up and we began to dance. I hoped and prayed my palms weren't wet.

Miss Minsham was a firm believer in traditional ballroom dancing. The academy even taught a class in it. None of this depraved and possibly obscene rock stuff for our headmistress. No sirree! Most of the tapes chosen for all our dances, Marylou had told me, were show tunes and stuff from the era of the big bands. That suited me just fine, since I'd rather sway dreamily with Hugo...Hugh...than gyrate and jiggle.

I don't know how long we'd been dancing, or what we'd been talking about when I came to, as it were, and looked around. I had no intention whatsoever of mixing with anyone else, and Hugh didn't seem to, either.

Pam tripped past my line of vision in the arms of an athletic-looking boy who was doing some pretty fancy dance steps, swirling her around, dipping her, flinging her out and pulling her back. I hoped the safety pin she'd stapled herself together with would hold up under the strain.

Pam rolled her eyes despairingly at me over her partner's shoulder, pointed to him and mouthed, "Ed Of The Eighteen Arms!"

Over in the corner by the stereo equipment stood Marylou, surrounded by a bevy of admirers who were twiddling dials and pretending to help her search for tapes. She hadn't even had time to come away from the microphone, poor darling, before they'd all hot-footed it in her direction.

Naturally she was too polite to tell them she wasn't in charge of the music for the dance. Knowing Marylou, she was probably afraid she'd disappoint them. "Such *nice* boys, Portia," she'd say. "They're trying so hard to be helpful!"

Romaine Slezak, who was *really* in charge of music, was at the refreshment table stuffing herself fit to bursting. Romaine, who was as thin as a whippet in spite of her chronic, mind-boggling caloric consumption, would rather eat than do just about anything, so it looked as if Marylou would be stuck in her corner all night.

I saw Dee dancing with a tall, thin boy who had sandy hair, horn-rimmed glasses and an intense, sincere expression on his freckled face. She seemed to be enjoying herself. At least she wasn't trapped with someone she didn't like, I thought. Dee always said she was looking for a boy with a good mind. Maybe he was discussing the rise and fall of the Roman Empire. That would simply make her night.

"There's no such thing as perfect happiness," Mom always says. "There's a worm in the heart of every rose."

I think she got that from some obscure poem. The business about a worm in every rose wasn't a botanical fact. I was sure about that because when I was little I once picked apart every rose in our garden to test her theory and only found a little green aphid or two.

I thought about Mom's worm, though, when we were jostled by the couple dancing next to us. I distinctly felt a sharp female elbow jab me in the ribs.

It was Raquel Finnerty, looking gorgeous as usual. Her partner was gazing into her green eyes like a chicken being hypnotized by a cobra. Raquel gave Hugh an appreciative once-over.

"Who's that?" Hugh asked.

"Nobody, nobody," I said hastily. Then, to change the subject, I said, "I'm a sophomore. How about you?"

"A junior. But this is my first year at Farnsworth."

"What a coincidence?" I cried delightedly. "So am I . . . new to this school, I mean. My, we certainly have a lot in common, don't we?"

"My father works for the State Department," Hugh explained. "We've lived all over and I've gone to more schools than I can count. We're living in Washington, D.C., right now, but Dad's due for another transfer soon. He and Mom enrolled me in Farnsworth because they wanted me to have the last two years of high school in one place, no matter where they went."

"How exciting," I said. "Moving around all the time."

"Not really. Sometimes I wake up in the middle of the night and I don't know where I am." Hugh stopped dancing and said, "Hey, it's warm in here, isn't it? Why don't we get some punch and sit out the next couple of dances somewhere cool?"

Before I knew it, he was taking me into the reception room. "No!" I said. "No. Not in there!" I grabbed his elbow, sloshing some of his punch onto the marble floor of the foyer.

Hugh bent down and mopped it up with his paper napkin. "Why not? What's wrong with it?"

"Well, er, we aren't usually allowed in there."

"It looks like they've opened it up for the dance. Come on, Portia. I'm sure it's okay."

I guess I could have made an issue of it, but that would have involved telling him about the ghost of the mad French maid and what had happened to me earlier in the evening. I didn't want Hugh to get the idea he'd been dancing with a lunatic, so I clenched my teeth and followed him into the room.

"It sure is cool in here, all right," he said. "Especially right over here, in front of the fireplace. Come on over here, Portia, and feel it. It must be a draft from the chimney. That's funny. It's been warm all day."

"Ah, ah, no. Let's sit over here, on the sofa," I said, picking a spot as far away from the fireplace as possible. I sat down and bounced up and down on the sofa a couple of times to show how comfy and inviting it was.

I'd read a lot of ghost stories. A cold spot was always supposed to indicate where *it* had happened— murder, suicide, mayhem, whatever. What if Mr. Seaforth had been standing in front of the fireplace when the mad French maid had zapped him? I could just picture it: Mr. Seaforth in a smoking jacket, the maid in her black dress, ruffled cap and apron. Her face would have been pale with emotion, her eyes large and staring. And then, as he clutched himself and fell, she would have turned the gun on herself and slowly, slowly...

I shivered and tried to take a sip of my punch. The glass beat out a woodpecker tattoo on my teeth. Hugh didn't notice. He was looking around the room.

I felt like an utter fool. Why was I doing this to myself? A vivid imagination can be a real curse. Dee was probably right. I did have an irrational fixation—don't ask me why—on that mad French maid.

But now that I, too, was in love, *really* in love, I could understand how she must have felt, and why she went insane with grief. Not that I'd go *that* far, mind you, if I were jilted.

"Poor thing," I murmured. "Poor thing. How she must have suffered."

At that, the craziest thing happened.

The light on the table by the sofa suddenly burned brighter, and I had the peculiar sensation of something warm and comforting brushing across my cheek. It was almost like a caress.

Strangely enough, it didn't frighten me, even though I couldn't explain what had happened or what had caused it. Or why it had happened at all. And the oddest part was that I discovered, to my surprise, that I'd lost my fear of the room and its sad secret.

"Did you say something? I couldn't hear you," said Hugh. "Did you see that lamp? The wiring in this building must be in bad shape."

I groped wildly for something to say, something normal and casual. "Why did your parents pick Farnsworth for your school?" I asked, blurting out the first thing that came to mind. "There must be any number of boarding schools in Washington."

Hugh drank his punch, placed the empty cup on the table and leaned back against the sofa cushions, putting his hands behind his head. "My mother's folks lived hereabouts at one time, and she'd heard about how good Farnsworth was. They were big landowners in the old days. Wealthy ones."

"Does your family still own any property in this area?"

"No. They lost just about everything in the Depression. The funny thing is, though, I could have been heir to this place."

"You mean the academy?" I asked. "What are you talking about? Did your family own it?"

"No. They didn't own it, but they nearly did. My great-grandmother was engaged to the old guy who built it. I can't remember his name."

"Your great-grandmother was engaged to Mr. Seaforth?"

"Yeah. That's who it was. Seaforth. Anyway, he died before they could get married."

He was shot before he could marry her, I thought. I almost said it aloud. Just then the lamp on the table rocked back and forth, its prisms jangling. It made a sizzling sound and went black.

"Boy, I'm sure glad I don't own this place," Hugh said. "It's a dump. Loose wiring and shaky floors. Did you see that lamp bounce around? They must be playing a fast one next door. Let's go in and give it a try."

I looked back over my shoulder as we left the room. The lamp had come back on.

Was I imagining things? Had it really been just loose wires and shaky floors? I tried to believe that that was what had caused it. But I knew Miss Minsham was a stickler for safety. Surely the building would have had to have been rewired in order to pass inspection when she had opened the school. And those floors were solid oak!

Now that the mad French maid knew Hugh was the great-grandson of her old rival in love, would she try to revenge herself on him?

There you go again, Portia, I told myself. You're making a big supernatural deal out of nothing.

Maybe.

Chapter Eight

When the dance broke up, Hugh asked me for my phone number and said maybe we could go to a movie the following Saturday night if I wasn't busy.

If I wasn't busy? Was Cleopatra too busy to date Mark Antony? Was Evangeline too busy for Gabriel? Was Elizabeth Barrett too busy for Robert Browning?

I smiled demurely and said that would be nice, and that I didn't think I had anything planned for next Saturday night.

"My roommate has a car," Hugh said. "We can double-date. I'll call you next week and let you know how everything works out."

In the entire history of womankind, the most beautiful words ever uttered by a boy to a girl have been, "I'll call you next week."

I floated upstairs to my room bursting to share the good news with my roommates.

They were waiting for me, eyes agog.

"Who *was* he?" Pam demanded.

"The search is over, girls," I said. "I've found Mr. Right!"

Glad cries were uttered on every side. I monopolized—well, they encouraged me to monopolize—the next half hour's conversation with ecstatic descriptions of Hugh: his looks, his adorable personality, his wit, his charm.

When I finally ran out of words to describe his perfection, I asked, "What about you three? Did you meet anyone?"

"I danced practically all night with a boy named Rusty Nolan," Dee said. "He was *so* interesting. Very intelligent. I really had a good time. And I think he likes me. He said he'd call."

More glad cries.

Marylou said she'd enjoyed herself, even though she hadn't danced a step. "Such nice boys. And so helpful. One of them even volunteered to teach me to play tennis tomorrow. Isn't that sweet?"

"He probably wants to get a good look at your legs," said Pam.

"And Harvey Snelling..." Marylou continued. "You remember Harvey Snelling? Well, he said his parents are coming down next weekend and he's invited me to go to dinner with them at the Horse and Hounds."

"Didn't I tell you, Portia?" said Pam. "They all want to introduce Marylou to their parents. No wonder. She's the kind of girl every mother wants her son to date. When they get a look at her, I bet they increase old Harvey's allowance.''

"You haven't said a word about your evening, Pam," Dee said.

"So what's to say? I spent the whole night in the clutches of Ed of the Eighteen Arms."

"I thought you didn't like him," I protested.

"I don't," said Pam.

"Then why did you hang out with him?"

"For the same reason Fay Wray hung out with King Kong. For the same reason kidnap victims hang out with their captors. He treed me like a possum!" Pam suddenly got very busy hanging up her clothes and getting ready to take a shower.

"But—" I began. Dee silenced me with a look.

When Pam had left for the shower room, I asked, "What's this all about, Dee? She said he was a passion-crazed beast. Why'd she spend the evening dancing with him?"

"I think Pam likes Ed Hogan, but she doesn't want to admit it," Dee said.

"How can she like a boy like that? Pam says she has to fight him off all the time!"

"You ought to know by now that Pam likes to dramatize herself, just for theatrical effect. If Ed Hogan ever really came on strong, she'd probably faint from shock."

"Ed Hogan is a very nice boy," Marylou said firmly.

"But what's all this stuff about him trying to drag her out behind the bushes last year at the Prom?" I asked.

"It was an azalea bush, Portia. One azalea bush. And it was only knee-high," Dee said. "What really happened was that Ed had a pebble in his shoe and he wanted to take it off without everyone seeing his sock. I think it had a hole in it or something."

"Ed Hogan is a very nice boy," Marylou said.

"Then why is Pam carrying on like that about him? I asked.

"Pam is all bluff and bluster," said Dee. "Underneath she's very insecure, I think, about boys. So if things don't work out between Ed and her, she wants everyone to think it's because she rejected him, not the other way around."

"Have you ever thought about being a psychologist, Dee?" I asked. "You'd be a whiz at it."

The next week flew by. Hugh called on Wednesday night and told me it was all arranged. We'd be double-dating with his roommate, the one with the car.

On Friday I received a letter from my mother:

My wonderful girl,

Your phone call Sunday afternoon came as an answer to my heartfelt prayers. Now I can sleep at night.

Yes, I know you told me in your first (*and only!*) letter that you liked the academy and that you had made friends, but I was afraid you were only being noble, that you were merely trying to spare me because of my delicate health.

By the way, in answer to your question, no, I have not had any vertigo attacks lately. I did have a mild asthmatic seizure last week, however, when Tess dyed her hair pink with my food coloring. She said it was for her role as the Sugar Plum Fairy in the *Nutcracker Suite*. Madame Slandowska assured me a sacrifice of that enormity was definitely not necessary. Anyway, I recovered nicely after Velda at the Pink Pamper returned Tess to her normal coloration.

But to get back to you, darling. The joy and happiness in your voice made me realize that Dad and I did, in fact, make the right decision about your schooling. We are pleased, too, that you had a good time at your school dance and that you have met a fine young man. But remember, Portia, you are at Miss Minsham's to prepare yourself for a useful, fulfilling life, and that your studies should and *must* come first!

We are all looking forward to Parents Weekend. Enid is eager to share her experiences at graduate school with you, and Tess wants to show you some new ballet steps.

As ever,
Your proud and happy mother

PS: I am now busy copying one of Monet's water lily paintings for my art class. My teacher assures me that words simply *cannot* express her feelings about my technique! *Voilà*!!!

I spent all of Saturday in preparation for my big date with Hugh Miller. I slept late with tea bags on my eyes. Then I got up, sat out in the sun to pick up a rosy, brimming-with-health look and spent the rest of the afternoon shaving my legs, fooling around with my hair and assembling the world's most perfect outfit.

Dee had a date with Rusty Nolan, and Marylou was going out with Harvey Snelling and his parents, so our dorm room was like backstage at the opening night of the opera. Piles of clothes were discarded on beds as we tried out different ensembles. Hair spray, perfume and floating bits of powder hung like a toxic cloud over our dressers, and you couldn't walk safely across the room without tripping over shoes that had been tried on and rejected.

In the midst of all this, Pam told us rather shame-facedly that she had a date with Ed of the Eighteen Arms. Only, and this was a shocker, she referred to him as Ed Hogan.

We all made a point of treating her announcement with elaborate casualness, as though Pam had never gone on and on about what a despoiler of pure young womanhood he was and how she couldn't stand him. Pam seemed relieved at our attitude, and before long she was her usual old self again, bossing us around and cracking stupid jokes.

When the call came on the intercom that my date was waiting to pick me up, I felt my knees buckle from sheer nerves.

Pam, Dee and Marylou told me that I looked gorgeous, that Hugh was a lucky guy and that I was going to have a marvelous time. That bucked me up. It's good to have a live-in support group.

As I left the room I heard Pam say to Marylou, "Ed Hogan had a big crush on you last year, didn't he?"

"He did *not*!" Marylou retorted. "Ed wants to get into TV work some day, he says, and he wanted me to introduce him to my mother, that's all. And besides," she added cunningly, "you're the one Ed Hogan has always had a crush on."

I smiled happily as I went down the hall. I hoped Pam would have as much fun on her date as I was going to on mine.

Hugh was waiting for me in the foyer. He was gazing up at the ceiling and checking out the roof beams, as if he were a building inspector in search of termites.

"Wow, Portia! You really look great!" he said as we walked down the front steps. "Josh's date is already in the car. I think she's a friend of yours."

And there in the front seat, with a smug smile on her face, sat Raquel Finnerty.

Chapter Nine

My evening was totally ruined, thanks to Raquel Finnerty.

The movie theater was in Warwick, a classy little town—village, actually—just a few miles down the road. It was the watering hole for the horsey set that lived nearby on large estates and regularly went fox hunting.

The main part of the town reflected the local mania for riding down and slaughtering innocent foxes. The inn was called the Lazy Fox. The leading boutique was the Foxy Lady. The beauty salon was named Fixin' the Vixen, and a gold-lettered sign over the local florist read Gone to Ground.

"I don't get the significance of that one," I said. "It sounds more like a funeral parlor than a florist."

Josh, Hugh's roommate, looked over his shoulder at me as he parallel-parked across the street from the

Tally Ho cinema. "Gone to Ground is a term used in fox hunting. It means the fox has taken to his den. You're right. It does sound like a mortuary, except that the people of Warwick are too important to die. They just prop them up in their saddles and no one knows the difference," he said with a wry smile.

I liked Josh. He was, as Marylou would have said, a *nice* boy. But what was a nice boy like Josh doing with a girl like Raquel Finnerty? He wasn't the one I'd seen at the dance gazing into her eyes; I hadn't seen him at the dance at all.

"I don't remember seeing you last Saturday night, Josh," I said as we all crawled out of his compact car.

"I wasn't there," Josh answered. "But if I'd known what I was missing, I would have come."

At first I thought he was speaking to me, but Raquel hopped right in and set the record straight. "You didn't miss all that much, Josh, honey," she said, laying on the smarmy charm for all she was worth. "And you don't have to come to a mixer dance to see me. All you have to do is call. After all, we are friends."

Maybe I imagined it, but she seemed to stress the word friends. Friends, as opposed to romantic interests. She did, and this I didn't imagine, flash Hugh a coquettish look as she said it, as though to indicate she was merely Josh's date, not his girlfriend.

Hugh gave her a foolish grin, and I just barely resisted the impulse to twist his arm.

"Raquel, you broke my heart in twenty-nine places last year," Josh said in a mournful voice, slipping me a quick wink. "I can't tell you how wonderful it is that you consider me a friend."

Raquel dimpled and preened.

I wondered what had happened last year. Poor Josh. Raquel had probably dazzled and then dropped him. Maybe she'd merely been cutting her teeth on him for practice. And now she was after bigger game. Hugh, maybe? No, not Hugh. He was mine!

Lookswise, Josh wasn't anything you'd write home about. He was of medium height with brown hair and eyes, not exactly what you'd call handsome. Still, there was something—well—interesting about him. He had a funny, offbeat sense of humor that I'd noticed on the drive into town. And I liked the way his hair curled on the back of his neck.

I can't remember the name of the movie we saw at the Tally Ho. It was just starting as we took our seats.

"Oh, we must sit boy-girl-boy-girl!" Raquel trilled out as we clambered into our seats. She saw to it that Josh went in first, then herself, with Hugh next to her and finally—naturally—me.

The story line of the movie ran something like this: A beautiful young housewife with a beautiful little daughter and a handsome young husband finds out she's dying of an incurable disease. The audience isn't told, specifically, the nature of the disease, but the heroine gives a plaintive little cough, cough, from time to time, which her husband doesn't seem to notice. This is just as well because the beautiful young housewife doesn't want him to know she's dying. She's saving that for the last reel. In the meantime she goes about finding a new wife for him, one who will be a good mother to her beautiful little daughter and a wonderful, kind, sweet wife to the handsome young husband.

It was corny, but somehow I imagined myself as the beautiful et cetera housewife with Hugh, of course, as the husband. The daughter even looked a little bit like Enid did in her baby pictures. Tears had begun to pool in my eyes and Hugh was furtively slipping an arm around my shoulders when Raquel had to go and spill her popcorn.

"Oh, my goodness me!" she said. "Aren't I the clumsy one!"

"Shh!" said the people in the row behind.

Hugh helped brush the popcorn off her designer suede skirt.

As for the movie, well, when the beautiful young housewife finally gets around to telling her husband that she's dying—dying, but all she wants is his future happiness—I was sniffling audibly. Hugh offered me his handkerchief with a gallant flourish. When I finished blowing, he tenderly took my hand in his, leaned over and—

"I can't see over the head of the man in front of me," Raquel said in a stage whisper. "I swear he's grown a foot since the movie started."

"Shh!" said the people in the row behind us a little more forcefully.

Hugh, being a gentleman, offered to trade places with her. As this was taking place, the people behind us, clearly at the end of their tethers, started moaning and yelling, "Down in front!"

I saw the rest of the movie with Raquel tucked next to me. I stole a glance at her. She looked like a cat that had just swallowed an extremely delicious canary.

After the movie we went for banana splits at the ice-cream parlor and then headed back to school.

"The academy's going to put on *Our Town* this semester," Raquel said brightly as we drove. "You guys ought to try out for it. I know I am!"

"What about you, Portia?" Hugh asked.

"I thought I might give it a whirl," I said. "I was in a couple of plays last year at Custisville High, and it was fun. Of course, I was only in the mob scenes."

"I was in the chorus of the musical Miss Minsham's put on last spring, even though I sing like a frog," Josh said. "You're right, Portia. It's fun to get on a stage and ham it up."

"That's where you and I met, Josh," Raquel reminded him.

"Yeah. How could I ever possibly forget?" said Josh.

For the second time that evening I wondered what the story was with Josh and Raquel. Josh certainly didn't act as if he was madly in love with her. In fact, several times I'd caught him looking at her sourly. But if that's how he felt, why had he dated her?

"If you try out, Portia," Hugh said, "I will, too." He tightened his arm around my shoulders. When he took my hand and squeezed it, I squeezed back. His face was close to mine, and the scent of his after-shave made me feel dizzy and fluttery.

"It's a deal, Hugh," I managed to say. "I hope we both get good parts."

"Well, then," Josh said. "I might as well have a go at it myself. Who knows? I might be another Laurence Olivier, waiting to be discovered."

"Oh, what fun!" cried Raquel, clapping her dear little paws. "The three of us, and Portia."

Mom always says it's a good thing we can't peer into the future because we might not always like what we see.

Boy, is she right.

Chapter Ten

In case you're wondering how crazy mad in love I was with Hugh Miller, I'll tell you.

I was so freaked out, bananas, bonkers, head over heels about him that without even trying I could hallucinate the sound of his voice. I'd totally forgotten about the ghost of the mad French maid and all the strange things that had happened in the reception room the night of the mixer.

But it all came back to me the following Wednesday.

I was on an errand to the office for Mr. Hamilton, our divinely handsome biology teacher. The fact that he'd singled me out to carry a message to Miss Minsham's office turned every girl in the class positively green with envy.

All classes were still in session, naturally. The halls were deserted and dimly lit, as usual. Miss Minsham had this thing about conserving electricity. She always turned out the main hall lights from the master panel in her office during class periods and switched them back on when she rang the bells for our breaks.

I was just raising my knuckles to tap at her door when a furtive movement over by the reception room caught my eye. It was Antoine, the creepy handyman. He was clutching a bouquet of red roses in his grubby hands and was starting to open the door to the reception room when he realized he was being spied upon.

His reaction was amazing, simply amazing. He jumped back guiltily and blushed. In the poorly lit hall he looked like one of those warning lights they put atop tall buildings so airplanes won't crash into them.

"Ah, *mamzelle*," he said in great embarrassment. I'd never heard him say anything before. His gentlemanly French accent, like Charles Boyer's in one of those old movies, surprised me. With a name like Antoine, I should have known he'd be French, but somehow I always figured he'd communicate in grunts.

"Ah, *mamzelle*," he repeated. "I was only carrying in the flowers. Madame Minsham she, uh, likes the bouquets in this room."

I knew for a fact he was lying through his teeth. Maybe because I figured someone as uptight about her electric bills as Miss Minsham wasn't about to go wasting money on roses, long-stemmed roses at that, in a room that was hardly ever used. I noticed, too, that Antoine kept glancing anxiously at the office door, as though he was afraid Miss Minsham was going to come barreling out at any moment and catch him in the act.

Why was Antoine bringing roses to the reception room? I'd never figured him for an amateur interior decorator. A paid assassin seemed more up his alley. Was it true what Mom always said, "You can't judge a book by its cover"? I hoped so. Then maybe I could stop picturing Antoine wandering the halls at night with a carving knife held aloft and poised for the strike.

I told my roommates about it later when we were in bed after lights-out.

"It doesn't surprise me that Antoine likes roses," Marylou said. "He's actually very nice, you know."

"What do you mean, nice?" I demanded. "What's nice about Antoine?"

Marylou heaved a patient little sigh. "Well, he covered for me once last year when I came in late for curfew. He was on porter duty and didn't report me. Now that's what I call nice!"

"You mean Antoine stands porter duty along with everything else he's supposed to do?" I asked. "That man is a real jack-of-all-trades. But I'd sure hate to meet him at the door in the dark of the moon."

"Here we go again, folks," Pam said, yawning as she flopped around in her bed and punched her pillow. "The trouble with you, Portia, is that you have this morbid fixation on ghosties and ghoulies and things that go bump in the night. Your mother must have seen too many horror movies when she was preggie with you."

"Preggie?" I echoed. "Preggie? If you mean pregnant, why don't you say pregnant?"

"Because preggie sounds nicer. And heaven knows we all want to be nice, just like Marylou."

"How'd I get mixed up in this?" Marylou complained. "I'm just an innocent bystandee!"

"Bystander, Marylou," corrected Pam. "The word is bystand*er*, not bystand*ee*."

"The final word on this is sleepy," grumbled Dee. "I'm sleepy. You're sleepy. We're all sleepy. Can we skip the usual semantic discussion just this once. Please?"

"All righty," Pam snickered. "Good nighty, sleep tighty."

It wasn't Pam's musical snores that kept me awake until the wee hours; it was the thought of Antoine sneaking into the reception room with those roses. Why had he acted so guilty? Why was he putting flowers in a room no one ever entered? Who were they for?

When I finally dozed off I dreamed of Antoine. He was putting roses—long-stemmed roses—on a grave. The grave of the mad French maid.

Chapter Eleven

Saturday morning of Parents Weekend dawned, as they say in novels, clear and bright. My alarm clock was set for six-thirty, but I didn't need it. From out in the hall came the thundering hoofbeats of the other sophomore residents as they scurried to and from the bathrooms. I was on my feet and rubbing the sleep from my eyes before my Baby Ben had a chance to sound its call.

Pam rolled out of bed and lay on the floor moaning. "What's all that running around I hear out there? Are we on the *Titanic* and we've hit an iceberg?" When she got no reply, she flung her arms and legs out in a spread-eagled position and launched into a mournful chorus of "Nearer My God to Thee."

Marylou was already up and pawing through her wardrobe. I noticed she'd made her bed. Marylou can move with the stealth of an Apache when she puts her mind to it.

"Will you please get up off the floor, Pam, before I step on you!" she demanded. "And get moving. We've got to clean up this room before our parents arrive. It looks like a pigsty!"

Dee sat up in bed, yawned and scratched her ribs. "Aunt Edna won't get here until about ten. What time are you all expecting your families?"

"Mama and Dash shuttled down from New York to Washington early this morning," Marylou said. "They're probably on their way right now in a rented car."

"Who's Dash?" Pam wanted to know. "Is your mother bringing a dog?"

"Dash Flambard plays a doctor on *Kiss Tomorrow Goodbye*. Right now Mama—her character, Lila Lamour, that is—is going blind and needs an operation. Dash plays Dr. Goodman."

"If she can't see, why are you so antsy about cleaning the room?" Pam said.

"Ha, ha. Very funny, Pam," Dee said. She crawled out of bed and began doing her usual early-morning calisthenics. "Dash Flambard is quite a name. Is he Hungarian or something?" she asked, puffing.

"Actually, it's just a stage name. His real name is Sheldon Krapowictz," said Marylou.

"Krapowictz?" put in Pam. "Krapowictz? Isn't that something contagious you get when you travel in Mexico? No wonder your mother's going blind."

Marylou ignored that one. "Mama seems really excited about Dash. Personally I think it's because she sees him everyday in his white coat and stethoscope. She's always had a mad thing about doctors. I wouldn't be a bit surprised if he turns out to be Step-daddy Number Five.''

"Well, tell her she'd better get a second opinion, take two aspirin and call you in the morning," said Pam.

Dee gave up on her exercises. "Oh, Pam! Don't tell me this is going to be one of your days! Can't you save all that sparkling repartee for your parents? I hope they get here soon and take you away. When are your folks arriving, Portia?"

"If I know my mother, she'll probably be one of the first to arrive. I bet she sat up all night studying *Bartlett's Quotations* so she can dazzle the members of the faculty."

I wasn't far wrong. Yes, Mom was one of the first to arrive. I didn't see Dad, Enid or Tess, but Mom was in the auditorium, and yes, she had a book tucked under one arm.

It wasn't *Bartlett's Quotations*, though. She'd been boning up on conversational French. I recognized the battered red book as the one Dad's Uncle Melvin brought back from World War II.

I should have guessed, I groaned to myself. Now that Mom was into her mad artist phase, she probably fancied herself a French linguist.

As I drew nearer, I saw that she had Madame Bonât, the French teacher, backed up against the marble fireplace and was asking her in ringing tones if there were any *Boche soldats* billeted in the village. I knew that sentence because Uncle Melvin used to tell us that was "pretty near the only thing" he ever learned to say in French.

When Mom saw me her face lit up and she released poor Madame Bonât.

"This *tête-à-tête* has been *très charmante, madame*," Mom burbled in parting. *"Adieu. Passez-moi le fromage."*

Madame Bonât looked dazed, but she managed a weak but gallant little wave of farewell. *Vive la France!*

"What was that *passez-moi* thing you said, Mom?" I gasped as she pressed me vigorously to her bosom with cries of motherly rapture. "What did you say to Madame Bonât?"

"I'm not too sure, but it might mean pass me the cheese," Mom chirped. "Oh, Portia! Portia, *ma chérie*, you look positively blooming!"

"Cheese? What cheese? I don't see any cheese?"

"Really, Portia," Mom said, giving me another bear hug. "You're such a little goose. Of course there isn't any cheese. But I pronounced it nicely, didn't I? My accent was Parisian. Pure Parisian. We don't want Madame Bonât to think your old mother isn't conversant with the French language, do we now?"

Dad, Enid and Tess were out in the garden beyond the library, standing under the striped awning of one of the tents that had been erected on the grounds. They were sipping fruit punch and spearing melon balls with colored toothpicks.

I've never been sentimental about my family, but I did get a pang—was it affection?—looking at them.

Tess was the first to spot me. She was standing in her favorite pose—shoulders back and down, toes pointing out at 180-degree angles. She always does this in crowds, so everyone will know she's a dedicated ballerina. She grinned when she saw me, the sun glinting on her orthodontistry.

Enid was her usual knockout self. Her pale blond hair was pulled back by an Alice band and foamed—

that's the only word to describe it—halfway to her waist. She was wearing a powder-blue cotton knit sweater and a thin, floppy skirt of the same color that molded itself to her snaky hips and long, slim legs whenever a breeze caught it.

Dad, as usual, looked charming, cheerful and slightly confused. I don't know what it is about my father, but people always seem to gravitate toward him. Maybe it's his face. He looks so kind and sympathetic or something. People always take one look at him and immediately begin to bare their souls.

To my horror, the person baring her soul, or at least chattering away to him, was none other than the exotic Mrs. Finnerty. I'd been hoping the Finnertys wouldn't come to Parents Weekend, and that I'd be spared the sight of Raquel for at least two days. Whatever Señora Finnerty was saying, Dad was nodding earnestly. Maybe she was telling him how cruelly I'd been persecuting her dear little daughter.

"Yoo-hoo, Richard!" Mom sang out. "*Regardez.* I've found Portia!"

Dad smiled from ear to ear when he saw me, and I had to swallow a funny little lump in my throat. Until now I hadn't realized how much I'd missed my impossible, weird, peculiar but lovable—yes, lovable, I had to admit—family.

We were all wallowing around in a lot of huggy-kissy, touchy-feely reunion stuff when I noticed that Señora Finnerty had slipped away and that Mr. Hamilton, the divine Mr.-Mel-Gibson-Himself Mr. Hamilton, was hovering on the edge of our group.

And guess who was the center of his bug-eyed attention? Guess who he was gazing at like one of King

Arthur's knights who'd just found the Holy Grail? Enid. My sister Enid, that's who.

Ye gads! I thought. What has Enid got? And why can't I have it?

"Oh, Mr. Hamilton," I said. Miss Minsham would have been proud of my good manners. "Have you met my family? My father and mother, Mr. and Mrs. Johnson. And my sisters, Enid and Tess."

For a wild minute there I was afraid Mr. Hamilton would sink to one knee and kiss Enid's hand. I mean, can you believe this? Mr. Hamilton, who could speak so cold-bloodedly about the mating habits of praying mantises, pink to the tips of his well-shaped ears over meeting my poopy sister Enid?

Enid, for the first time in her scholastic, nunlike life looked impressed. Definitely impressed. And excited. I could see the pulse begin to throb in her throat.

"Oh, yes, Mr. Hamilton," she stammered. "You're Portia's, ah, Latin teacher."

"Biology teacher," Mr. Hamilton corrected lovingly, devouring Enid with *those eyes*. "Biology."

I suddenly realized I had a lot to learn about sex.

Somehow Mr. Hamilton, with his raggedly breathed "Biology," had managed to convey the impression he was Rhett Butler about to sweep Scarlett up *those stairs*!

As for Enid, well, for once she seemed to be thinking about something besides the flowering of the Elizabethan sonnet. She was looking at Mr. Hamilton as though she'd just found Mr. Goodbar. It was embarrassing. That's what it was. Embarrassing.

All the world loves a lover, as the poet says, except when it happens to be your older sister and your biology teacher who are sniffing and circling each other.

Mom and Dad didn't seem to notice anything unusual. They're such innocents. They probably thought that Mr. Hamilton was just being hospitable. I hope I never live to be as old as they are. Boy, when I have kids, I'll know exactly what they're up to.

We probably would have stood there forever, Tess plopping melon balls into her mouth and Mom and Dad carping away about how picturesque the grounds were, what lovely weather we were having, et cetera, et cetera, while Enid and Mr. Hamilton breathed on each other like a couple in a Certs TV commercial, if my roommates and their families hadn't converged on us.

Marylou's mother looked just like Marylou. If Marylou were twenty-five years older, that is, and wore spiky black false eyelashes and lots of pancake makeup.

"Oh, my!" Mom gasped when she laid eyes on her. "It's you! Lila Lamour! You poor dear thing! What are you doing out of the hospital. I thought you were going bl—"

"Mother," I said calmly, although internally I was dying of humiliation. "Lila Lamour is just a character in a soap opera. Mrs. Maloney merely plays her. She isn't really going blind."

I hoped I was right in calling Marylou's mother Mrs. Maloney. What with four ex-husbands, who knows what her real name was? Even Marylou said she sometimes forgot how to address her letters home.

Mom blinked and flushed a bright red. I think she was more embarrassed because she'd tipped her hand about watching soap operas than for her goof. She always says that soaps are trashy and that she wouldn't be caught dead watching them.

Dash Flambard stepped gallantly into the breach. The name Dash Flambard definitely suited his looks better than Sheldon Krapowictz.

"Marylou has told us so much about Portia, but I never dreamed she had such a lovely mother and sisters."

"Merci bien," Mom simpered, full of herself again. "You are *très, très* flattering."

Dee's Aunt Edna was short and plump and perspired a lot, but it was easy to see that she thought the sun rose and set in her niece.

She told us she ran an antique store in Leesburg, Virginia, and hoped to pick up some interesting pieces in a couple of wayside stores she'd passed on her way to Miss Minsham's.

"That reminds me, ha, ha, ha," piped up Pam's father. "You know the definition of an antique, don't you? An antique is a fugitive from the junkyard with a price on its head!"

Aunt Edna smiled gamely, but Mrs. Shultz laughed uproariously at her husband's wit.

"Jerry's a proctologist," she told Aunt Edna by way of explanation. "You ought to hear all the naughty jokes he tells about that occupation. My Jerry is a real Steve Martin."

It was easy to see where Pam got her demented sense of humor. No doubt about it, Dr. Shultz would be a real hit on "The Gong Show."

Aunt Edna was fanning herself agitatedly with her handkerchief and Marylou's mother was attempting to steer the conversation into more cultured channels when Pam pulled me away from the group and hissed:

"What's going on between your sister and Mr. Hamilton?"

"Did you notice it, too?" I whispered back.

"Notice? Notice? What's not to notice? Mr. Hamilton looks as zonked out as one of his chloroformed frogs! Why didn't you tell us your sister is absolutely, incredibly stunning? I think old Blue Eyes has finally bitten the bullet!"

"You don't mind, do you? I mean, I always thought you had a mad crush on Mr. Hamilton."

"Oh, give me a break, Portia, puh-lease. I'm not psychologically ready for older men yet. I was just re-hearsing my emotions, you might say, for when I meet my one-and-only. I thought you knew that."

"Well, then . . ."

"This is rich, Portia. Really rich," exulted Pam. "That I should live to see the day when the original immovable object meets the legendary irresistible force. When I write up the results for science, they'll probably give me the Nobel Prize!"

I never got to take Enid on a tour of the building. Mr. Hamilton did that.

And when we four roommates and our families went to dinner that night at the Horse and Hounds, Enid was noticeably absent. She had a hot date with Mr. Hamilton.

Chapter Twelve

Romance was in the air, no doubt about it.

As I told my roommates the following week, when we were supposed to be doing our homework: "Isn't it amazing that we've all got love interests? I mean, I've got Hugh. You've got Rusty Nolan, Dee. Pam's got Ed of the . . . Ed Hogan, that is, and . . ."

Pam smiled graciously. Now that she'd come out of the closet about Ed Hogan, she even had the nerve to violently deny that she'd ever said mean things about him.

"And Marylou has Harvey Snelling," I concluded.

"I don't know if I've got Harvey Snelling, exactly," Marylou said doubtfully. "It's more like I don't want to hurt his feelings."

Pam rolled up the essay she'd been working on and tooted into it. "And—ta! ta!—Enid's got Mr. Hamilton, our man for all seasons."

"That's right," I said.

The upshot of the discussion was the agreement that yes, we four were really living life to the fullest, Harvey Snelling notwithstanding.

I got a letter from my mother the following Friday:

Portia, *ma chérie*,

Miss Minsham's Academy has turned out to be everything I hoped it would be. To see you there in the garden, your hair blowing in the breeze (are you using a good conditioner, Portia? I think you have a few split ends), your eyes alight with *joie de vivre*, made me realize that your dear father's and my financial and emotional sacrifices on your behalf have not been made in vain.

Enid behaved quite oddly, even for her, on the way home. Tess says (get ready for a big surprise!) that Enid is in love with that nice biology teacher of yours. But, *mon Dieu*, when did it happen??? Surely my motherly instincts would have alerted me to any vibrations passing between the two of them. You know how amazingly observant I am when it comes to you girls.

This is really quite unusual for Enid, isn't it? It's hard to imagine her in love with anyone who hasn't been dead for four hundred years. But who knows? *C'est la vie!* What a shame they are geographically so far apart, now that Enid's back at school in Massachusetts. Well, if it's true love, love will find a way.

Speaking of motherly instincts, Dad said he had a nice chat with a Mrs. Finnerty. Do you know her daughter? Her name is Raquel, Dad says.

Anyway, Mrs. Finnerty is apparently concerned because Raquel doesn't seem to have many friends at school. Is she shy or introverted or something? Perhaps you could include her in some of your activities. Bring her out of her shell, as it were. As that wonderful, wonderful poet (what's his name?) said: "No man is an island." We pass this way but once, darling, and it's our duty to help our fellow traveler.

Must dash!

Love,
Mother

Ha! I thought. Raquel Finnerty shy and introverted? That would be the day. And she didn't need to be brought out of any shell. She belonged behind bars, that's where she belonged.

I had to admit I was feeling more hostile than usual toward Raquel. Tryouts for *Our Town* had been held the night before, and Raquel seemed a shoo-in for the role of Emily, the romantic lead.

Raquel was a good actress. Naturally two-faced, for starters, she could lie like a trooper. So when she got up on the stage, batted her big green eyes and launched into this big speech Emily has—she'd even memorized it—you'd have to be blind not to see that the part was hers.

"Hey!" Hugh said, clapping enthusiastically as Raquel hopped down from the stage. "She's really good! You're really good, Raquel!"

Hugh and Josh and some other guys from Farnsworth had come over for the tryouts. Hugh and Josh were sitting with me. We'd already been up.

Raquel trotted over to us and sat down. "Did you really think I was good, Hugh?" she asked. "I was so nervous!"

Nervous my foot, I thought. I'll just bet she was nervous up there hogging the limelight.

"Quiet in the audience!" roared Miss Columbo, the head of our speech department and director of the play. "I want you back onstage, Hugh, for another reading. Come on, come on, we don't have all night."

I leaned over and whispered to Josh, "I think Miss Columbo wants you for one of the bigger parts. I saw her write something next to your name when you read the part of Emily's father."

Josh shook his head. "Just my luck. A middle-aged man. Maybe that's why girls always think of me as a friend instead of a lover. It's my fatherly qualities."

I didn't know what he meant by that. The more I saw of Josh, the cuter he looked to me. Of course, he couldn't begin to compare with my Hugh, but I didn't see why Josh couldn't get any girl he wanted.

Josh was looking at me as though he wanted me to say something, but I couldn't think of anything appropriate, so I changed the subject.

"Hugh reads very well, don't you think? I wonder what part he'll get. I'm sure it'll be one of the leads."

Josh gave me that funny look again. "Hugh does everything well. He's what I'd call a real winner. You didn't do half-bad up there yourself, Portia. I didn't know you had all that talent."

"I asked for quiet in the audience, and anyone who can't keep his or her mouth shut will be asked to leave!" Miss Columbo yelled, giving Josh and me the evil eye. Miss Columbo didn't need a megaphone. She had what show biz people call "excellent voice projection."

Hugh looked like a matinee idol up there on the stage. He was wearing a white V-necked tennis sweater and slim-legged denims. His dark wavy hair gleamed in the overhead lights. My pulse rate jumped at the very sight of him.

He certainly had star quality, I reflected dreamily. And it wasn't just because I was prejudiced, either. Hugh was the most gorgeous boy I'd ever met.

Beside me, Raquel leaned back in her seat and crossed her legs. Her eyes had an odd, speculative look, like that of a Bengal tiger pondering its next meal.

Suddenly I sat bolt upright and my palms went clammy from sheer fright. If I didn't get a part in the play and Hugh did, Raquel would be with him every night during rehearsals. I wouldn't even be able to see him. Noncast members weren't supposed to hang around when play practice was going on.

Well, I got a part all right. That of Mrs. Webb, Emily's hardworking, middle-aged mother, along with Josh as Emily's father.

And Hugh got the part of George Gibbs, Emily's sweetheart.

And Raquel, hammy, sneaky old Raquel, got the stellar role of Emily Webb, one, I was sure, she'd play to the very hilt.

Life is a jungle.

Chapter Thirteen

Along about the second week of play practice, Raquel started calling Hugh "Hughey." Sometimes she called him "George," and that was even worse because she pronounced it "Jaahge." The play was set in New Hampshire, and Raquel was doing her darnedest to sound like a New Englander. She'd even gotten into the habit of saying "ayah" when she meant "yes," just like that old geezer in the Pepperidge Farm commercials.

She was perfectly disgusting.

What was even more disgusting was the wedding scene, where she and Hugh, as the newly married couple, went into a big clinch. The stage directions said, "Kiss is held throughout following speech," and the speech, as delivered by Ned Gooch in the role of Stage Manager, seemed to go on forever!

Fortunately Miss Minsham came tiptoeing into the auditorium one evening during the wedding scene and issued new stage directions.

"A casual embrace is all that's necessary for this scene, Miss Columbo. You may omit the prolonged kiss."

"But the author indicates—" boomed Miss Columbo.

"I don't care what the author indicates, Miss Columbo. Consider this discussion at an end."

Hooray for good old Miss Minsham!

Being with Hugh every night wasn't turning out as I'd expected, either. We never had a chance to talk, really talk. He was usually onstage with Raquel. When I was onstage, it was more often with Josh.

And when I wasn't onstage, I was in the back of the auditorium scribbling away at my homework. I couldn't let my grades go down just because I was in a play.

Josh was fast becoming a true-blue friend. He'd sit with me and help me translate Caesar's *Commentaries*, or he'd explain the poetry of Emily Dickinson to me for my English class. Things like that.

Up until now I hadn't realized how smart he was. Hugh told me Josh was an honor student, but I'd assumed he had to grub for it. Instead, Josh seemed to be able to skim-read, close the book and know everything he was supposed to know.

"How do you do it?" I asked one night.

"Do what?"

"Get good grades without really trying."

"Oh, that. My mom and dad are both teachers. And my big brother's a brain. I'm just a good listener. A lot of this stuff I've heard over the dinner table."

"You're just being modest, Josh."

"And you're being nice, Portia." He touched my cheek with his fingertips. Did I imagine it, or did he let his hand linger on my face longer than was necessary?

"That's what I like most about you, Portia. You're so . . . so . . . nice."

"You're starting to sound like Marylou," I said, laughing.

"Marylou who?"

"You know. Marylou, my roommate. She thinks everyone is nice. That's her favorite word."

"I'll bet she uses it a lot about you," Josh said.

"Silence in the back of the auditorium!" Miss Columbo yelled. "Keep it down! There's a rehearsal in progress, as if you didn't know!"

More and more I was becoming obsessed about Josh and Raquel's relationship. What had gone on between them last year? Was he still in love with her or what?

The four of us were still double-dating on the weekends, but Josh didn't seem to be noticeably turned on by Raquel. And, more and more, Raquel seemed to be coming on to Hugh.

I tried to tell myself that their roles as Emily and "Jaahge" would, naturally, cause a certain amount of bonding—I believe that's the term. But, to tell the truth, I was beginning to lose a lot of sleep over their special little inside jokes and the way Raquel always managed to sit next to Hugh in the movies, at the soda shop, et cetera.

I was surprised to see that it didn't bother Josh. He acted as if he almost enjoyed it. One of these days, I promised myself, I'd ask him how he felt about Raquel, but the opportunity never seemed to present itself.

Once again I'd almost forgotten about the ghost of the mad French maid, until one night Pam cornered me in the shower room after play practice and said, "I apologize, Portia for doubting you. Something strange *is* going on with Antoine."

"What are you talking about, Pam? It's late and I've got to get to bed."

"Listen to this," she said, toweling her hair furiously. "This afternoon in the music room I had a voice lesson that went overtime. So I had to go to Miss Minsham's office for a chit because I was late for my next class. And there he was!"

"Who?"

"Antoine. He was sneaking into the reception room with a bunch of carnations on his arm."

"Carnations?"

"And that's not all. He was carrying a black candle."

"Black candle? Where'd he get a black candle? I've never seen a black candle before."

"Good grief, Portia. Don't you ever read trashy novels? Black candles are what they use for voodoo and exorcisms and stuff like that."

"Are you telling me . . . ?"

"I sure am. Antoine looked guilty as sin. I know I've always made fun of you with your ghost stories about the reception room, but you just might be onto something."

"What? What am I onto? What do you suppose is going on with Antoine and the reception room?"

Pam stopped toweling her hair and looked me straight in the eye. "I've come over to your side, Portia. I'm not laughing anymore. Think about this. Antoine is French. The mad maid was French. Antoine's been sneaking into the reception room with flowers and black candles. Black candles are definitely not the norm. Now, what in heck do you suppose Antoine's up to?"

"Are you trying to tell me—"

"You bet your sweet patootie I'm telling you," Pam said. "Dollars to doughnuts, Antoine's trying to exorcise the ghost of the mad French maid."

Chapter Fourteen

Mr. Hamilton looked perfectly awful. His blue eyes had a bleached, bleak look to them and his manly cheeks had lost their usual rosy color.

Pam elbowed me in biology class and passed me a note that said, "Mr. H. looks like he has a terminal disease."

I wrote back: "Can it be love?"

"If this is love, I hope I die an old maid," wrote Pam.

A letter from Tess explained the whole situation:

Hi Portia!

Mom asked me to write you, so here goes.

The hot news around here is Enid and that cute biology teacher of yours. Their romance is really big time. BIG TIME, Portia. Just like Romeo and Juliet. We told you last week when you called how Mr. Hamilton (his name is Alan, in case you didn't know) has been phoning Enid every night long-distance and sending her flowers and telegrams and cards and all that junk and how Enid's been sending him love poems that she's written herself. I can hardly believe all this.

Well, what you don't know is that he flew up to Massachusetts last weekend to see her. It was really something. Enid called and told us about it and she was crying to beat the band!!! I think she's flipped her lid. I've never known Enid to go bazoo before.

Anyway, what happened is that Alan banged on her door at midnight last Friday and actually got down on his knees and asked her to marry him. I wish I could have been a mouse under the table for that scene!

And—listen to this, Portia—Enid said yes! Enid the ice maiden. Yes, she said. Oh yes, yes Alan darling. Yuk!

But before you run over to the biology lab and kick your way through a bunch of dead gerbils and amoebas to congratulate him, wait till I tell you the rest of the story.

After Enid said yes, oh yes Alan darling, our future (maybe) brother-in-law, the male chauvinist pig oink oink (more on that later), said let's get married right away Enid my beautiful beloved. Let me carry you off to old Virginney to my darling little one-bedroom cottage in a town I (Tess) have never heard of. I think it's called Warwick. Have you ever been there? It sounds like Nowheresville to me.

I might not be quoting the conversation exactly, because Enid was practically babbling when she called and Mom's been a basket case ever since. So I might have to take a few liberties here and there. Even Dad's nerves are shot to heck. He's broken out in an attack of shingles. I hugged him yesterday and he screamed with pain.

Anyway! Enid said to Alan, but what about my graduate degree program Alan darling? And Alan darling said to heck with your graduate program Enid my silly little pussykins or words to that effect.

Then Enid said what do you mean to heck with my graduate degree program? It's my life. And Alan said love is more important than higher learning for a woman. He said, we'll live in my picturesque little vine-covered cottage and you'll learn to cook and to sew, you're gonna love it I know.

And then Enid said I will not Alan darling! I want my master's degree. I want my Ph.D. I want to be a college professor. And that's when the old sand hit the fan.

They had a terrible fight Enid said. An 8.2 on the Richter scale fight. Enid says she's in love, really truly in love and that Alan is the only man she will ever care for etc. etc. but what about her? What about her future career? And how can Alan be so blind and unfeeling? Oh what am I to do, oh what am I to do she kept asking Mom.

It's a real mess around here, Portia. I mean it's really *bad*!!! Thank God for my ballet lessons. They get me out of the house.

Mom is in such a state that she chopped up her water lily painting. She said she needed to actualize her feelings of frustration. The painting wasn't all that great but what the heck, she liked it.

Now all Mom does is sit around the house looking like a pretzel in what she says is the yoga lotus position. She's searching for wisdom, she says, and spiritual enlightenment. If you ask me, I think she doesn't have any idea what to tell Enid. I know she'd love to see her married off and producing (horrors!) grandchildren, but she'll also die if Enid doesn't get her Ph.D. You know what a *thing* she has about higher education.

Well, that's about all the news as of this minute. Mom wanted me to let you know what was happening because she said her psychic energies were too low to take pen in hand and it's such a hassle trying to phone you at the dorm.

Love,
Tess

PS: Boy, was this ever a long letter. I can hardly uncurl my fingers.

PS again: Mom says to call her collect.

Ye gads! I thought. What next? I was still sitting at my desk, clutching Tess's letter when my roommates came skipping in.

"You look ghastly, Portia," Dee said. "What happened?"

I sat them down and read them Tess's letter from beginning to end. There was a stunned silence when I finished.

"That Tess writes a fast-paced letter," Pam said at last. "A real page-turner. Has she ever considered writing paperback romances?"

"I think I'm going to cry," said Marylou. "Oh, this is terrible. Terrible. And they were such a perfect couple."

Dee didn't say anything. She just sat and thought. Her eyes dart around when she's thinking a problem through. Then she usually spits out a brilliant answer, just like a computer. The three of us sat there, watching her. The suspense was unbearable. Finally the oracle spoke.

"I think everyone in your family is overreacting to this," Dee said. "What I mean is, they're operating strictly on their emotions right now, not on common sense."

"Exactly what do you mean by that?" I asked a little huffily. I knew my family was a bit scatty at times, but I didn't want anyone else to say they were.

"Now, Portia, I'm not putting your family down. I just mean that everything has happened too fast for them to cope with at this point."

"Okay. I'll go along with that," I said, mollified.

Dee waved her hands around expressively. "This whole thing was too sudden. Crash, Enid met Mr. Hamilton and it was love at first sight, like a bolt from the blue."

"That's how I want it to be for me someday," Marylou said dreamily.

"Then, crash! They court madly through the mails and over the telephone for a couple of weeks."

"Yes," I said. "But—"

"And then before you know it, Mr. Hamilton is pounding on Enid's door at midnight and getting down on his knees...on his *knees*, Portia! The man is obviously a mad romantic, and he's out of his head over Enid."

"Sniffing formaldehyde does strange things to the brain," volunteered Pam.

"So what are you trying to say, Dee?" I asked.

"What I'm trying to say is that your family simply ought to settle down and take things one day at a time and think the problem through. Actually, it's Enid's problem and she has to think it through. Women have careers and marriage and children nowadays. Why can't Enid? Mr. Hamilton is certainly intelligent enough to realize that. He and Enid don't have to get married right away. In fact, they shouldn't."

"They could live in sin," Pam suggested hopefully.

Dee shot Pam a disgusted look. "I'm not saying that. I just don't think Enid and Mr. Hamilton ought to rush into any permanent decisions until they get to know each other better and sort out their priorities. Why can't Enid continue on and get her master's degree this year? Then, maybe next year, Mr. Hamilton could get a job teaching in Massachusetts, or Enid could go to the University of Virginia for her Ph.D. They could take it from there."

What Dee had said made great sense—I mean, about Enid and Mr. Hamilton taking their time and not rushing into things until they had their future worked out. Dee made it all seem so simple. Why hadn't I thought of that? Why hadn't Enid? My mother surely hadn't.

"Are you positive you're only fifteen years old?" I asked Dee. "How come you're so smart so early in life?"

"It's just because I'm emotionally removed from the problem, that's all," Dee explained. "I think your family at this particular moment is too close to the forest to see the trees."

"That's a great saying," Pam said. "May I write it down in my notebook? How do you spell forest?"

"I'm serious, Dee, when I said you ought to be a psychologist," I said. "You really ought to think about majoring in psychology when you go to college."

Pam went into her mad German act. "Und maybe study in Wienna, Austria, eh? Und maybe liff in zin mit Herr Doktor Zigmund Freud, eh? *Ach der lieber!*"

Dee threw a book at her and missed.

I wanted to talk to Hugh that night, just the two of us. I wanted to tell him about Enid and Mr. Hamilton and everything that had happened. Our relationship was never going to get off the ground if Hugh and I didn't learn early on to share things and to, well, communicate!

The horrible thought crossed my mind that so far we'd never communicated, really communicated, about anything, and that all we'd ever shared were a few hot and heady kisses in the back seat of Josh's car. Come to think of it, we hadn't even done much of that recently. Raquel Finnerty always managed to horn in at the crucial moment.

I was feeling down when I went to the play rehearsal, and I guess it showed.

When Hugh and Raquel were onstage rehearsing the famous soda fountain scene, where Emily and George begin to realize they're in love, Josh took me out to the hall and sat me down on the pink marble steps. With a little coaxing, he got the whole story from me—Enid and Mr. Hamilton's fight, what Dee had said and how I felt about Hugh and me and Raquel.

"Dee's right, you know, about your sister. Don't worry, Portia. Everything will work out for Enid and Mr. Hamilton. Building a loving relationship takes a lot of time and patience and getting to know each other."

He patted my knee. "And don't give up on Hugh. If he has any sense in that good-looking head of his, he won't want to let a girl like you get away from him."

How could I be so madly in love with Hugh Miller, I wondered, when it was Josh Devlin I was beginning to admire?

Chapter Fifteen

The long-distance calls I placed collect during the coming week must have had all the stockholders of AT&T dancing in the streets. Never before had I done so much reaching out and touching someone.

"Oh, Portia!" Enid wailed. "You must be the sweetest little sister any girl ever had! Imagine you and your friends sitting down and trying to figure out a solution to my problems!"

"Well, as Dee says, you don't have to hurry up and make any big decisions right now, Enid. This is the rest of your life we're talking about. I'm sure you and Alan can work things out."

"I hope so. But you don't know how obstinate and impossible he can be at times."

"Are you kidding? He's my biology teacher, remember?"

"How does he . . . Alan . . . look? Does he seem upset?"

"Upset is hardly the word for it. He looks like utter heck! And I think he's lost at least ten pounds."

That seemed to cheer Enid up considerably. She sounded almost perky when we hung up.

Maybe it was the connection, but when I talked to Mom she seemed to be sort of intoning her words instead of speaking them. And she said things like "Allah willing" and "so let it be written," and used lots of quotes from Omar Khayyám and a book called *The Prophet*.

I noticed she'd stopped speaking French.

"How wise you are, my child," Mom said in her strange new voice. "What you say is laden with wisdom, much wisdom, far beyond your tender years. Yes, undoubtedly Kismet has brought Enid and Alan together and the path of their love will be made smooth. The bird of time has but a little way to fly and, lo! the bird is on the wing!"

That was the gist of my many telephone calls to Enid and Mom. Pam swore I was spending so much time in the phone booth that I might as well bring in a hot plate and a sleeping bag.

Tess wrote:

Portia, oh moon of my delight,

Mom's been acting so goony and far out around here lately in her search for inner peace that I guess it's catching. But I think she's finally simmering down. She had to take Omar and *The Prophet* back to the library and she's beginning to run out of quotes. Thank heaven! If she'd mentioned that Moving Finger Having Writ business one more time, I'd probably have given *her* the Moving Finger. Burn this letter!!!

And she threw her back out doing one of her yoga things so at least I don't have to come home from school anymore and find her on the floor all twisted up in some freaky position. It was really embarrassing when I had a friend with me.

Dad's shingles seem to be clearing up, too. This attack seems shorter than the ones he's had before. But then time always goes by fast when you're having fun, doesn't it? Poor old Dad. What has he ever done to deserve an eggcentric wife and three crazy daughters? (Did I spell eggcentric right?)

As Enid probably told you, Alan is flying up to Massachusetts again this weekend. He must be spending a fortune on airplane tickets. I thought teachers were supposed to be underpaid.

Anyway, Enid says he told her he's been doing a lot of thinking lately about their future and that maybe it's time he came into the twentieth century. Considering the fact that the rest of us are getting ready to move into the twenty-first century, he's still running late.

Oh well. The leaves of life keep falling one by one. (I don't know what that means, but it's been number one on Mom's hit parade these days.)

Love,
Tess

PS: I wish you all would give me a chance to come on the phone one of these times. I *hate* to write letters!!!

Now that things were moving along nicely at home, I could get back to my own problems. Pam was currently playing the role of Nancy Drew and was shadowing Antoine.

"I told Ms. Gebhardt it was, you know, *that* time, and that I couldn't participate in PE this week. She thought I was going up to my room with a hot water bottle, but instead I hung around outside the reception room today in hopes of catching Antoine and his black candles."

"Did you see him?"

"Not hide nor hair. And Lord knows Antoine has enough hide and hair to outfit a zoo."

"What will you do if you do see him?"

"I'll simply play it by ear, Portia. You know what a creative genius I am."

The thought of Pam bursting in on an exorcism in progress was simply too much to be borne. "Maybe you ought to let him perform an exorcism or whatever you call what he wants to do. Wouldn't we all be better off without a ghost?"

Pam mulled that one over for a second or two. "I'm a seeker of truth, Portia. If something funny's going on, I want to know! Which reminds me . . . how come I'm doing this all alone? It's *your* ghost. And besides, I've only got a week. Any longer and Ms. Gebhardt will think I'm a biological curiosity. Why don't you take next week? Maybe we can get Dee and Marylou to get out of PE the following two weeks."

"What makes you think Antoine's going to do his thing during PE period? Why not at night or something?"

Pam gave me a superior smile. "Elementary, my dear Portia. It's the only time, don't you see? PE is always the last period of the day and everyone is out of the building, on the athletic field, in the gym, the stables, et cetera. That's when Miss Minsham locks herself up in the office, supposedly to go over records and do her correspondence, but personally I think she takes a nap. She has a comfy recliner in there.''

"But what about at night?"

"There's always a porter on duty at night. And everyone's using the front door. No, Portia, according to my scientific deductions, PE period is when Antoine will try to do *it*!"

Dee and Marylou weren't too happy about being dragged into the investigation. They finally agreed, although Marylou said she didn't like it one tiny bit because Antoine was a very nice man, a lovely, kind man, and she felt simply awful spying on him. And how could she get out of PE when everyone knew she never had That Kind of problem?

"Ye gads," Pam said. "Can't you pretend?"

On the third day of Pam's stakeout, she reported excitedly that Antoine had gone into the reception room with a big bunch of gladioli.

"What happened?" I asked.

"Have you ever tried looking through a keyhole, Portia? All I could see was Antoine's back. He was fiddling around with those flowers and he was talking to himself. Well, actually, I think he was talking to the fireplace."

"He was talking to the fireplace? What did he say?"

"I don't know. That door is pretty thick. Suddenly Miss Minsham popped out of her office and asked me what I was doing and why wasn't I in PE? When I told her, she made me swallow a couple of aspirin tablets and sent me to my room. She made so much noise that

Antoine must have heard her, because while I was swallowing those pills, I saw him slither out of the reception room like a snake and beat it out the front door.''

And on the fourth day of Pam's investigation, Miss Minsham caught her again. She told Pam in no uncertain terms that Pam was supposed to be either in her room or at PE, and furthermore, in the future, she would keep her door open and anyone found loitering in the halls would get ten demerits.

"So there goes the case," Pam said dismally.

"Not really," I said. "If we can't come and go in that area during PE, neither can Antoine."

"I'm glad," Marylou said that night after lights-out. "I wasn't cut out to be a Sam Slade."

"It's Spade, Marylou. Sam Spade," Pam said.

"Oh, please, God, no! Don't let them start arguing over words when I'm trying to get to sleep," Dee pleaded.

Dead silence.

"Thank you, God," Dee said.

"It's Sam Spade, Marylou," Pam said. "Not Slade!"

The next evening at play practice, Miss Columbo announced in her usual bell-like tones: "Since we cannot function properly with everyone not on stage chattering away in the back of the auditorium, those awaiting rehearsal will be allowed to sit in the reception room and practice their lines!"

Chapter Sixteen

Hugh, Raquel and I were in the reception room. Everyone else was either onstage or in the dining hall. It was the last week of rehearsal, and Miss Columbo said we'd be working late. Dinner had been served in two shifts, since the boys in the cast would be taking their evening meals with us for the next few nights. Raquel was practicing her big finale.

"Could you keep it down, Raquel?" I said. "I'm trying to do my homework."

"You'd be better off if you practiced your lines," she shot back at me.

I no longer feared the reception room. If the ghost of the mad French maid was still hanging around, she was friendly, at least to me, anyway. Hugh always complained of a chilly draft when he stood by the fireplace. But then he was the great-grandson of the debutante who'd chiseled in on Mr. Seaforth's affections, so naturally Hugh would be receiving negative vibes when he stood on the spot of the murder-suicide.

"Now where was I?" Raquel wailed. "Portia's broken my mood!"

"You've broken Raquel's mood, Portia," Hugh said accusingly. "Go on, Raquel," he prompted. "And Mama's sunflowers..."

"It's no use," she said, pouting. "I've lost my momentum. Portia's always doing that."

"You're always doing that, Portia," Hugh said.

"I don't know what gets into her," said Raquel. "A person would think she's jealous of me or something."

"Now what could *you* possibly have that I'd be jealous of, Raquel?" I said from between clenched teeth.

Raquel looked from Hugh to me with a sly smile. "There you go again, Portia, picking on Raquel," Hugh said. "What's the matter with you? Why are you always picking on Raquel?"

So, the moment of truth, I thought. What I'd been afraid would happen was finally out in the open: Hugh and Raquel, together, against me.

Things had been going from bad to worse with Hugh and me the past couple of weeks. He and Raquel always seemed to be off in a corner somewhere, just the two of them. I'd begun to feel like a third thumb. And tonight was the last straw.

I had the sudden, terrible urge to put my head down and bawl all over my history notes, but I managed to control it.

The lamp on the sofa table flickered several times and made little sizzling sounds.

I could see now that we three had been working toward this moment from the start. All those dates, when I'd been foolishly happy just to be with Hugh, even though he and Raquel, I remembered now with an awful clarity, were always looking at each other over the back seat of Josh's car, sharing private jokes.

And then the play. What an idiot I'd been to think that it would be my big chance to get close to Hugh! Instead it was Hugh and Raquel, George and Emily, the couple of the century.

If you've ever been on the outside, eating your heart out, looking in on all the togethers, you'll know how I felt at that moment. I felt betrayed and abandoned, and unloved. I felt ashamed, too. Maybe it was my fault, I thought. Maybe I wasn't pretty enough, or interesting enough. Maybe I didn't wear the right kind of clothes. Maybe it was my personality—did I laugh too much? Did I laugh enough?

No, I told myself angrily. There's nothing wrong with me! I am what I am, and if Hugh prefers Raquel, then he can have Raquel!

I put my books to one side and stood up slowly. "I'd like to speak with you, Hugh," I said quietly. "Alone."

Hugh looked at Raquel. She shrugged her shoulders and left the room.

Now, there's real communication for you, I thought bitterly. Those two don't even have to talk to each other. They've got a Morse code thing going with their eyes.

Hugh and I were alone in the room.

The lamp wobbled again on the table and made more hissing sounds.

"Why didn't you tell me long ago that you liked Raquel?" I asked.

"Of course I like Raquel," Hugh said evasively. "She's a great girl."

"That's not what I mean."

"What do you mean?"

"I mean, why didn't you tell me that you like—as in love—Raquel?"

"You're playing this scene kind of heavy, aren't you?" asked Hugh.

"Answer my question."

"Raquel's right, Portia. She always said you were the jealous type. You've always been jealous of Raquel, haven't you? What are you trying to do?" Hugh demanded. "And who do you think you are, anyway? We've dated a few times, that's all. What makes you think you own me? You don't own me. So goodbye, Portia, and lots of luck." He walked over to the sofa and bent to pick up his sweater.

That's when it happened.

The light bulb on the table lamp gave a loud pop, and little bits of glass flew in all directions.

Hugh stood there staring. I was glad to see he still had both his eyeballs. Shards of glass lay on his sweater. He even had some in his hair. He wasn't bleeding, though. As far as I could see, he didn't have a scratch on him.

"What are you, a witch or something?" he asked as he stomped past me, brushing himself off. He nearly knocked me down in his haste.

I just stood there after he slammed the door, not moving. All those things they say in romance novels about people's hearts breaking are true. I could actually feel an achy sort of pain in the region of my heart.

I prodded myself gingerly. True, we'd had hot dogs and sauerkraut for supper and I was now tasting them for the second time, but I was definitely not experiencing indigestion. It was a broken heart, all right. My idol had just shown that he had feet of clay. My dreams of everlasting love with Hugh Miller had just turned to garbage. My life was over. Over.

Well, maybe it was over.

It was over, wasn't it?

No, doggone it, it wasn't over! Why should my life be over because of someone like Hugh Miller?

Suddenly I thought about that light bulb popping in his face. The door opened and Josh stuck his head in. "Hurry up, Portia. You're wanted onstage." He broke off when he saw my face. "Gee, Portia, are you okay? What happened?"

Chapter Seventeen

"Where are you going?" Josh called after me as I ran from the room. "You're supposed to be onstage."

"Do me a favor, would you, Josh? Tell Miss Columbo I'm sick or something. Make it sound good. I won't be back at rehearsal tonight!"

"But...but...Portia!" Josh sputtered. "What's happening?"

I didn't stop to explain. I left by the front door and sprinted across the cobblestoned parking lot toward the gym. At one time it had been a huge carriage house, then a garage, before Miss Minsham had converted it into a gymnasium. There was a small apartment over the far end, with its own outside stairway. Antoine lived there.

I took the stairs two at a time and hammered on Antoine's door. Lights were burning in the apartment, and I could hear the sound of canned laughter. Antoine was evidently watching a TV sitcom.

Still in his usual grubby work clothes but shoeless, he finally appeared at the door. He had a big hole in one sock, and a toe protruded. *"Mamzelle!"* he cried in alarm. "What is it? Did Madame Minsham send you? Is there an emergency?"

"No, Miss Minsham didn't send me, but yes, there is an emergency. May I come in?"

Antoine opened the door. I followed him into a small, untidy sitting room. He snapped off the TV and hastily began to pull on his shoes.

"What is the nature of this emergency?" he asked in that surprisingly cultured French accent of his. "To which part of the building should I present myself?"

"Actually, Antoine," I said, flopping down, unbidden, in a scruffy armchair. "It's a personal emergency."

Antoine stopped lacing up his shoes and eyed me suspiciously. "An emergency of a personal nature? Then why, may I inquire, *mamzelle*, have you come to me?"

"Because you're the only one who can tell me everything I need to know about the ghost of the mad French maid," I said.

Antoine turned pale. At least I think he turned pale. Under all that facial hair and grime it was hard to be certain.

Antoine started to protest. "I? A ghost? What would I, a mere—how do you call it?—handyman know of any ghost?"

"You can cut the innocent act," I said. "The jig is up, Antoine."

"Eh?" he said, honestly puzzled this time, so I translated:

"Please don't pretend you know nothing about the ghost of the mad French maid. I think she's haunting the reception room. And I think you have something to do with her. A friend and I have seen you going into the room with flowers and black candles. Black candles, Antoine," I repeated forcefully.

He uttered a despairing little Gallic moan and hunched over in his chair, covering his face with his hands.

"I want you to tell me all about it," I pursued. "Everything. What's your relationship to the mad French maid? And just what are you doing with those flowers and black candles? Are you trying to lay her spirit to rest?"

Antoine finally emerged from behind his hands. "It's a long story, *mamzelle*."

"Please call me Portia, now that we're cohorts and all," I urged.

"Very well, Portia," he said. "I will tell you everything, just as you have requested. Clotilde Beauvoir was my great-great aunt. She was the beloved and very beautiful sister of my great-grandmother. Our family comes from Marseilles, which, as you probably know, is a seaport. People travel from Marseilles to all parts of the world. When Clotilde was a young girl, not much older than you are now, she dreamed of going to America. My family tried to discourage her, but she would not listen to their warnings. And then, one day, when she had saved enough francs for the voyage, she left."

"And came to Virginia?" I asked.

"No. Not at first. At first she went to New York, but she did not like it. The noise, she said in her letters, and so many people speaking English at once confused her."

"So how did she wind up in Virginia? And out in the country?" I prompted.

"Mr. Seaforth was an acquaintance of the woman in whose house Clotilde worked. A kind woman. When she learned that Mr. Seaforth was looking for servants to staff his beautiful, great home in Virginia, she told Clotilde, because she knew Clotilde was unhappy in New York."

"If she knew Mr. Seaforth, who was evidently a real fink—a bad man—why did she let Clotilde work for him?"

"Mr. Seaforth could be very charming. It seems he had fooled her in regard to his real nature."

"Oh, I see," I said. "So Clotilde came to work for Mr. Seaforth."

"Clotilde was so happy. She wrote my great-grandmother many letters telling her of the house and its fine gardens. And then . . ."

"And then?"

"And then she began to write only of Mr. Seaforth. How handsome he was. How attracted to him she was. But she believed he would never return her affection because he was a great man and she was only a maid—a servant—don't you see?"

"Yes. But he did fall in love with her, didn't he? Or at least he pretended to. I mean, I heard they had a real romance going."

"Ah, yes. As I have mentioned, Clotilde was a beautiful young woman, open, honest and trusting. Naturally that *cochon*, that pig, Seaforth would see she loved him and take advantage of her innocence and inexperience."

"You mean he ... ?"

"Exactly. He told her he loved her. He even suggested—the liar!—that he might marry her some day. Clotilde was in ecstasy! She wrote her family, saying the man she loved, loved her. And that he had promised to marry her. But my great-grandmother knew it would come to misfortune."

"How did she know that?"

"The women of my family are very—what is the word for it?—knowing of the future."

"Knowing of the future? Do you mean they're fortune tellers or something?"

"Sometimes they have visions ... dreams ... that come true. And in these dreams they can see what lies ahead. They can also see what happened in the past. Secret things."

"If Clotilde had this gift, couldn't she see what would happen to her and Mr. Seaforth?" I asked.

"She was in love. Love makes a woman blind to many things."

"That's for sure," I said grimly, thinking about Hugh Miller. "So what happened then?"

"Her last letter, which my great-grandmother received after Clotilde's death, was full of despair. In it Clotilde said she had heard that Mr. Seaforth had promised himself to another, a silly, selfish young lady from a wealthy family. Clotilde said she was on her way to confront her lover, to persuade him he must marry her. She was desperate, you see, because she felt she had been dishonored."

"Oh, that *cochon* Seaforth!" I exclaimed indignantly. "So she shot him when he refused to marry her?"

"That is what they say," Antoine told me. "But my great-grandmother saw the happening in a vision. Clotilde did not murder Mr. Seaforth. She threatened him with one of his pistols, to be sure, but it was just to frighten him. When he attempted to take the weapon from her, it went off, killing him. She was so horrified she then quickly turned the gun on herself."

"So Clotilde wasn't a murderess after all," I breathed. "I'm so relieved. I hated to think of her as a cold-blooded killer."

"And now you know the story," said Antoine.

"Not all of it," I reminded him. "What about you? What are you doing here? And what's with the black candles?"

Antoine took a deep breath. "A year ago I was working in the Caribbean, on the island of Martinique. I have lived in many places and can do many things. I, too, wanted to see the world."

"Martinique? That's a long way from Virginia."

"Yes. Well, one day last year I received a letter from my grandmother. She has the family gift of seeing visions. She said Clotilde had appeared to her and told her that her soul was weary of being between this world and the next and wished her spirit could be set free. Because of her suicide, you see, which is a great sin because it throws away the most precious gift of all, life, she was forced to remain here, in this place, where she had committed her terrible crime against nature."

"But what did your grandmother expect you to do?"

"She said that if I came here, to the estate, the way would be made clear for me."

"Did it? Become clear to you, I mean?"

"No," Antoine said miserably. "I have been here many months and have tried everything I know, but Clotilde still walks."

"You mean, you've seen her? You've actually seen her?"

"Not really. But I can feel her presence."

"Listen, Antoine. Don't give up. Keep at it. That poor woman needs help, and it looks like you're the only one who can do the job. You're bound to hit on the right formula one of these days. After all, your grandmother says you will. It's just a matter of time, isn't it?" I tried to sound cheerful and optimistic.

Antoine shrugged. His shrug could have meant anything from "You might be right" to "Oh, heck, what's the use."

I felt better now, though, about Hugh and me. At least I hadn't shot him. I certainly wasn't as desperate as poor Clotilde had been. You know that saying about crying because you have no shoes and then meeting someone with no feet? That's how I was feeling. I knew now that I could face Hugh and Raquel without a lot of heartburn and tears.

I got up from my chair and turned to go. "You have a nice smile, Antoine," I said at the door. "You know, if you shaved off your beard and got a haircut, you'd look a lot like that French movie star—oh, what's his name—Yves Montand. Yes, that's his name. Yves Montand."

"Me? Look like Yves Montand?" Antoine chuckled. "You are most kind, Portia."

I could still hear Antoine laughing as I went down the stairs.

Chapter Eighteen

See? Didn't I tell you Antoine was a nice man?"
Marylou said, honking into a soggy Kleenex. "But,
oh, that poor Clotilde. Poor, poor thing! It makes me
want to cry!"

"Makes you want to cry?" Pam echoed incredulously. "You've been sobbing nonstop for hours.
That's the last dry tissue in the room, by the way. I
hope you're not going to start blowing your nose on
my sheets."

Pam's digital clock clicked over to 11:34. Have you
ever noticed that when you look at a digital clock upside down, the numbers become letters of the alpha-
bet?

The four of us were sitting on Pam's bed. We'd been
talking ever since I'd burst in on them, straight from
my interview with Antoine. I'd told them everything
that had happened, from my big blowout with Hugh

to Antoine's amazing story of Clotilde and his futile attempts at ghostbusting.

Dee didn't say much. Her brown eyes darted around the way they did when she was deep in thought. Finally she sighed and said, "This is absolutely incredible. To think I didn't believe you at first, Portia, when you said the reception room was haunted. But you've been right all along."

"And aren't we lucky to have such a fun roommate?" Pam said. "You've given new meaning, Portia, to the term 'adolescent emotional disturbances.' Up until now, my big fear was pimples on prom night. Now I'm starting to worry about stress-induced heart attacks."

"As I see it," continued Dee, ignoring Pam's usual theatrics, "we have to take this problem one step at a time. First of all, Portia, there's the matter of you and Hugh."

"Hugh the Phew!" sneered Pam. "What a jerk!"

"Hugh Miller is *not* a nice boy," said Marylou firmly. "Imagine him throwing Portia over for someone like Raquel Finnerty. Why, that's . . . that's . . . tacky!"

Tacky was Marylou's ultimate put-down.

No matter what the future brought, I'd always love Marylou for saying that. And Pam, for her Hugh the Phew. And Dee for wanting to help me sort out my problems. When you had three good friends in your rooting section, what more did you need?

"Are you sure you aren't heartbroken?" Dee asked with a worried frown. "You really thought the world of Hugh."

"I was wrong," I said. "Maybe it was just his fantastically good looks that made me fall for him in such a big way."

Pam spoke with great authority. "It was simply a matter of hormones. At this stage in our lives we have to beware of runaway hormones. They can lead to all sorts of horrible mistakes."

"You might be right, Pam," I said, thinking it over. "The first time I met Hugh something inside me went boing! Maybe it was just a case of—what did you call it?—runaway hormones. I didn't know anything about him, but my hormones went boing, boing! We never were good friends, now that I think of it. We never really talked together about anything important. We never really shared our feelings. It was just hormones going boing, boing in the back seat of a car."

"I don't understand this conversation at all," Marylou protested. "Hormones? Hormones going boing, boing? My hormones have never gone boing, boing over anyone."

"If by anyone you mean Harvey Snelling, you're not abnormal," Pam reassured her. "What self-respecting hormone would ever go boing over Harvey Snelling?"

"Oh," said Marylou. "I was beginning to get worried."

"Well, now that that's settled," Dee went on, "what should we do about Clotilde?"

"If you're going to suggest we hole up all night in the reception room and wait for her to appear, count me out," Pam said. "Miss Minsham would catch us, sure as shooting."

"This is just terrible, terrible," snuffled Marylou, searching in the rubble for a usable Kleenex. "That poor, dear Clotilde, doomed to wander forever and ever."

"But that's just it," I said. "She won't! Antoine said his grandmother the prophet, or whatever she is, told him that everything would turn out right."

"How?" Dee asked.

"Who knows? But his female relatives seem pretty accurate with their visions and things. So we can just relax."

Little did we realize it would be Raquel Finnerty, not Antoine, who would be instrumental in the laying of the ghost of the mad French maid.

Chapter Nineteen

Our Town was scheduled for only two performances, an afternoon matinee and an evening show, both held on Tuesday, the last day of school before the Thanksgiving break. Since Miss Minsham's was a boarding school, and holiday transportation to and from home had to be taken into consideration, we had Wednesday off and didn't have to be back at school until the following Monday.

The afternoon matinee was for the members of the student body, and any parents who arrived early to fetch their daughters. The evening performance was for families arriving later, and for the local gentry who, believe it or not, were big on homegrown theatricals.

Mom had written that my family, including Enid, would be there for the evening performance. Now that

Enid's big crisis seemed to be resolving itself, Mom sounded more like herself:

> ...then on to a little *après-théâtre* repast at that darling Horse and Hounds, a good night's rest (I've booked two rooms—you girls will have to share one of them) and home we merrily go, over the river and through the woods, for a lovely, old-fashioned Thanksgiving!
>
> What a thrill it will be, darling, to see you treading the boards, as they say (*and* playing a stellar role) in one of the great classics of the modern stage!!! My cup runneth over!
>
> I do hope you aren't nervous about it. *Are* you nervous, Portia dear? Remember—a case of pre-curtain jitters is perfectly normal and will serve to *hone* the fine edge of your performance. Even the theater greats suffered from it, so you will be in good company. Did you know that George M. Cohan used to throw up in a bucket on opening night, just before he strutted onstage? So you see...

Et cetera. Et cetera.

I was glad to see that Mom had her old fire back and was being her usual indomitable self, but I wished she hadn't gone on so about the possibility of me being nervous. Up until now I hadn't given stage fright a thought. I'd had too many other problems. But there's nothing like someone telling you not to be nervous, to make you nervous.

On Monday, the day of dress rehearsal, I woke up with a knot in the pit of my stomach the size of a ball of yarn. Just like George M. Cohan, I reflected.

"What if I twitch and tremble up there tomorrow?" I said as I brushed my teeth. "And what if I really get nervous and upchuck onstage?"

Pam patted my back reassuringly. "Just pretend it's part of the script. Do it like a New Englander from good old Grover's Corners and no one will know the difference. For such," she intoned, striking a pose, "is the magic of the theater!"

I started to laugh and got toothpaste up my nose. It burned, but my stomach felt better immediately and I knew I would be okay.

That morning Mr. Hamilton looked as if he was the one with a bad case of stage fright. He dithered around the biology lab like an expectant father who had just found out his wife was having triplets. I noticed he'd gotten a haircut so he'd look good for Enid. But in his current state of high anxiety over their coming reunion, he'd come to class with little patches of toilet paper still sticking to his face where he'd nicked himself shaving.

Pam smuggled me a note: "If he's this keyed up today, he'll be a real basket case tomorrow when your sister arrives."

I wrote back: "Would it help, do you think, if I told him Enid dyes her eyelashes? Or that she breaks out in hives periodically?"

"Probably not" was Pam's response. "As the poet says, 'The eyes of love see only with the heart.'"

Monday afternoon until dress rehearsal was free time for the members of the cast. We were supposed to get our costumes in order and have one last crack at studying our lines.

The boys from Farnsworth Prep arrived after lunch. I decided I'd keep my distance from Hugh Miller.

True, our love affair, if you could call it that, was ended, but I was still afraid I might be tempted to strangle him with my bare hands.

"What happened the other night, Portia?" Josh asked me. The two of us were sitting in a secluded corner of the reception room. "You were terribly upset. I've been worried about you. All Hugh will say is that the two of you have broken up."

"Josh," I said. "If I told you, you'd probably think I was flat-out crazy."

"No, I wouldn't. Try me."

I looked at Josh. How strange, I thought. At first he'd seemed so...well, so...ordinary-looking. But in the past few weeks I'd begun to notice how cute he was. Maybe not spectacularly cute like a movie star, or like Hugh Miller—may he'd go bald on his twentieth birthday—but cute in his own way. He had nice eyes, and kind of a sexy mouth that always seemed to curl up in a smile. And he had a clean, strong jawline. His nose had a funny little hump in it that sort of suited him. And I'd always liked the way his hair grew on the back of his neck.

"Try me, Portia," Josh urged again. "I won't think you're crazy. I think you're just about the most wonder...the sanest girl I've ever met."

"Are you sure you won't laugh, or jump up and call for the men in the little white coats?"

"Scout's honor," he said.

So I told him everything. And I mean everything. My feelings about the mad French maid. Hugh and Raquel. Antoine's story about Clotilde. Everything.

"Wow!" he said.

"Do you think I'm off my rocker?" I asked.

"No," he said thoughtfully. "No. I've done a lot of reading about supernatural phenomena. My grandmother came from England. That's what first got me interested in the subject. When I was growing up, she used to tell me all sorts of stories about strange happenings in those old English houses. I just never realized it could happen here at Miss Minsham's."

"Are you saying you believe me?"

"Yes. Yes, of course I believe you. I just wish you had told me all this before. But . . ."

"But what?"

Josh bit his bottom lip and blushed. Then he blurted out, "But are you sure you aren't still carrying the torch for Hugh Miller?"

"I'm telling you about the ghost of the mad French maid, and you're asking me about Hugh Miller?"

"You're darn right I'm asking you about Hugh Miller!"

"Why?"

"Why? Are you blind or something, Portia? I've had this thing about you from the very first time we met. You're beautiful. And smart and funny and nice and . . . and . . . well, I think you're just great," he finished lamely.

Me? Beautiful?

The eyes of love see only with the heart, Pam had said just that morning. And Josh—dear, sweet Josh— was seeing me with his heart. He actually thought I was beautiful! Not just beautiful but funny and nice and, well, just great!

"Oh, Josh," I sighed.

"But all the girls fall for Hugh. What chance have I got when a girl like you meets a guy like him?"

"Wait a minute, Josh," I said. "I thought you were mad for Raquel Finnerty. Now there's a beautiful girl."

"Me? Raquel Finnerty? Are you kidding?"

"You and Raquel have always been a twosome," I persisted. "All those dates you had with her!"

"Last year, when I first met her, sure, I thought she was something special. But it only took one evening listening to her prattle on about herself and I knew she was a real nothing. A self-centered, conceited nothing."

"Well, then, will you please tell me why you've been dating her all this time?" I inquired coldly.

"For a smart girl, you're really dumb, Portia," Josh retorted. "Why do you think I've been dating Raquel? I mean, really think about it! So I could be with you, that's why. Even though you've been mooning like a sick goose over Hugh, I wanted to be there, just to look at you and talk to you."

I broke out in a silly grin from ear to ear.

"What's so funny?" Josh asked crossly. "I haven't said anything funny."

"Oh, Josh," I sighed happily. "It's just that we're having our first lovers' quarrel already."

At this point, and speak of the devil, who came bouncing into the room but Raquel Finnerty herself, trailed by Hugh Miller. Now that they'd gone public about their flaming romance, Raquel was making it clear that Hugh was definitely her property. All he needed was a ring through his nose.

"Look everybody," she sang out in bell-like tones, waving a huge shopping bag around as if it were Old Glory. "I've been shopping in the village, and I found the darlingest dress to wear tonight when Hughey takes me *out to dinner*!"

She aimed those last three words at me with a look of pure malice. Hughey had never taken me out to dinner.

"Well, I'm not going to chauffeur them," Josh told me in an undertone.

"Love will find a way, I'm sure," I whispered back.

It was a good feeling to look at Hugh and not go all trembly in the knees. As a matter of fact, I was actually beginning to feel sorry for him. Poor Hugh. Hugh the Phew.

Raquel was pulling things out of her shopping bag. Some of the girls gathered round to see what she had bought. "And a new pair of dress pumps," she was saying. "And look, a bottle of that *terribly* expensive French shampoo with the *divine* designer scent. I believe I'll just run upstairs right now, quick as a bunny rabbit, and wash and blow-dry my hair so I'll look nice for my date tonight with Hughey when he takes me *out to dinner*. Hughey just loves my hair."

"I just love Raquel's hair," echoed Hughey, the henpecked robot.

Just then Miss Columbo called us all into the auditorium for some last-minute directions. She finished with, "And I want everyone back here in one hour. One hour, not a minute later, in complete costume for rehearsal!"

Josh walked me to the girls' dressing room behind the stage and gave me a quick hug before we parted. "You'd better get started on your makeup right away." So had I. It takes time to draw in all those wrinkles and powder your hair gray."

"Will you love me in December like you do in May?" I asked, mugging and crossing my eyes.

"I think it can be arranged," Josh said with a cheeky wink.

Miss Sturgeon was in the dressing room, helping out with the makeup. She was her usual bundle of nerves. A couple of girls who were in the cemetery scene were already at work on their faces. Others began drifting in.

"Where's Raquel? Where's our star?" whinnied Miss Sturgeon, wringing her hands.

"I think she's upstairs, washing her hair," said Patsy Duncan.

"Washing her hair? Washing her hair?" shrilled Miss Sturgeon in alarm. "If that isn't just like Raquel! She's supposed to be getting into her costume and makeup."

"Oh, she'll be ready in time, I'm sure," Patsy said reassuringly. "She's a real pro when it comes to slapping on makeup. And no wonder. She practices her technique all the time. She must fix her face every hour on the hour."

Patsy Duncan is a real kindred spirit, I thought.

When Patsy and I were all painted up in wrinkles and crow's-feet and buttoned into our granny dresses, the two of us went into the auditorium together. The male members of the cast were ready and waiting. Patsy and I went over and sat down with Josh and Ned Gooch.

"I just love mature women," Josh said with a senile leer, pretending to tremble. Josh looked pretty cute as an older man.

There was still no sign of our beloved leading lady when Miss Columbo stomped into the auditorium, knocking over several chairs. She was as noisy with her feet as she was with her mouth.

"Is Raquel still getting made up?" she hollered.

"Yes, where is she?" Hugh whined anxiously.

Yikes! I thought. What has Raquel done to that boy? Lobotomized him or something?

"Where's Raquel?" boomed Miss Columbo again. "What's keeping her? We can't start without her!"

A couple of seconds later we *all* learned where Raquel was.

At first I thought it was an ambulance siren—high, ululating whoops that kept getting closer. But when she kicked open the auditorium door, the whooping turned into shrill, hysterical screeching. She must have been hitting high C, because my eardrums popped. It was a good thing there wasn't a chandelier in the building, or she would have shattered every prism.

At first sight of her everyone in the auditorium froze, just as in that kid's game of Statues. And no wonder—Raquel was a sight to curdle milk. Her eyes were bloodshot and rolled insanely in her head. Something white and frothy hung from her upper lip.

It was only shampoo lather, as it turned out, but my first thought was: she's got rabies! She's foaming at the mouth and she's come to bite me!

Raquel stopped screaming and tore the towel from her head. Her wet hair came tumbling down. Literally. Some of it fell on the floor. And that's not all. It was green. Not a pleasant, woodsy shade but a bright, *Erin go bragh*, Saint Patrick's Day kelly green.

"Look!" she shrieked, holding up one lank strand. It came loose from her scalp and hung limply from her palsied fingers like a dead mouse. A long, skinny dead mouse. A long, skinny, *green* dead mouse.

That set her off again. "I'm ruined!" she shouted. "Ruined! And *she* did it!"

Raquel was pointing directly at me.

Chapter Twenty

For once Miss Columbo was speechless.

Raquel's screaming must have roused the entire school, because heads were hanging over the minstrels' gallery, peering down into the auditorium. I could see Mr. Hamilton among them, his toilet paper patches still intact.

Miss Minsham sailed into the auditorium and plowed through the gaping throng, which parted before her like the waters of the Red Sea opening up for Moses and the Israelites. "What's the meaning of this?" she demanded. "I will not tolerate this sort of behav—"

She stopped dead when she saw Raquel. Her mouth fell open, and she did a double take that would have been the high point in the career of any TV comic. "R-

Raquel," she stammered. "Wh-what have you done to yourself, child?"

Raquel treated herself to another ear-shattering wail. "*I* didn't do it," she sobbed. "*She* did it. Portia did it, that rotten jealous little..."

And then Raquel launched into a lengthy soliloquy, calling me a number of colorful and evocative names. She even brought my mother and the conditions surrounding my birth into it.

Miss Minsham, having pulled herself together, stepped forward and did the only thing the headmistress of a posh boarding school could do, given the circumstances. She slapped Raquel smartly. First on one cheek, then on the other.

Raquel hiccuped once or twice. She was a terrible sight. "Portia did it," she whimpered at last. "She hates me. She's always hated me. She hates me because she's a—" her voice gathered strength "—because she's a rotten, jealous little b—"

Miss Minsham let her have it again. "You're hysterical, dear," she said calmly. "Now get hold of yourself and tell me what happened."

"I bought the shampoo," Raquel said, mopping her nose with the sleeve of her white custom-made terry cloth robe. The little blue monogram on the pocket bounced erratically with every heave of her bosom. "I left the shampoo in the reception room when Miss Columbo called us into the auditorium. Then I went back, picked it up, went upstairs and washed my hair. But look at me..."

She started to work herself up into another frenzy, took one look at Miss Minsham's clenched fists and changed her mind.

"And just what has Portia to do with all this?" queried Miss Minsham crisply.

"Isn't it plain as the nose on your ugly old face?" Raquel screeched, forgetting herself. "Portia slipped into the reception room while I was gone and put something...something awful...lye or dye or something...into my shampoo."

Miss Minsham turned her attention to me. "What have you to say for yourself, Portia?"

"Miss Minsham," I said, taking a deep breath, my entire life flashing before my eyes. "This is insane. In the first place, how was I to know Raquel was going to buy a bottle of shampoo and leave it in the reception room? In the second place, where would I get lye or dye or whatever it was that turned Raquel's hair green and made it fall out? And in the third place, I was with someone from the time we left the reception room until now. They can vouch for me."

"That's right," Josh said, stepping forward. "Portia was with me. Miss Columbo called us all into the auditorium and then I walked Portia to the dressing room."

"And I was with Portia in the dressing room," chimed in Patsy Duncan. "We got made up and changed into our costumes and came back, together, to the auditorium."

Miss Minsham looked at me hard and appraisingly. Then she gave a little nod. It was settled. The verdict was in.

"Raquel," she said. "It seems highly unlikely that Portia had anything whatever to do with your... unfortunate condition. The fact that you would accuse a classmate of such a thing, and the ill-chosen epithets you have used in doing so, are a disgrace to the honor and tradition of this academy."

Raquel appealed to Hugh. "Tell them, Hughey. Tell them how jealous Portia is of me because I took you away from her."

Hugh sidled away from Raquel as if she had leprosy and he was afraid of catching it. "Leave me out of this," he bleated. "I didn't have anything to do with it."

"But, Hughey," protested Raquel.

"I don't know what you're talking about," Hugh insisted. "I thought we were all friends, you and I and Portia. That's all. Friends."

When the going gets tough, I reflected, the tough run like rats. And, oh, what a rat you are, Hugh Miller! How could I ever, *ever* have thought I was in love with you?

"I think you'd better come to the infirmary with me, Raquel," Miss Minsham said, putting her arm around Raquel's quivering shoulders. "I'm sure Nurse Evans will be able to help you." She looked up at the minstrels' gallery and noticed the faces peering down in horrid fascination. "Back to your rooms, everyone," she snapped. "Thanksgiving holiday doesn't begin until four o'clock. In the meantime, classes are in progress as usual."

As Miss Minsham left the auditorium with Raquel in tow, Miss Columbo, a broken woman, said in a pitiful whisper, "Oh, what am I to do? I've lost my leading lady. Oh, what am I to do?"

Chapter Twenty-one

Nurse Evans, who knew absolutely everything about the human body, said that Raquel would regain her hair. "A short haircut, two hundred strokes every night with a natural bristle brush and in a few months," she proclaimed, "Raquel will be as good as new."

On Tuesday, the day of the performance in which she was to have made theater history, Raquel slunk home in the back of her parent's Silver Cloud Rolls-Royce. It was rumored that Raquel had left Miss Minsham's never to return.

I watched from an upstairs window and saw Raquel, wearing a turban, get into the car. Miss Minsham, gallant to the end, stood by, obviously saying kind, sympathetic things because Mrs. Finnerty embraced her warmly before taking her place in the front seat.

As the car pulled away, Raquel rolled down the rear window and threw a shoe at Miss Minsham. Miss Minsham ducked nimbly and, as the Rolls disappeared down the driveway, she appeared to dance a triumphant little Irish jig. Then she sedately straightened her collar and cuffs and returned to the building.

True to the traditions of the stage, the show did go on. Patsy Duncan, it turned out, had played the part of Emily in a junior high school production and knew all the lines. Since her present role had been a minor one—one of the dead people in the cemetery scene—there was no casting problem.

The afternoon matinee went like clockwork. Patsy was great. Hugh, I must say, played his part rather shamefacedly, but perhaps the author had intended the character of George to be a humble one. As Miss Columbo always says, it's all in the interpretation.

I was resting up in my room, still in costume and makeup, before the evening performance, when my roommates entered.

"Portia!" Dee said. "You were absolutely wonderful!"

"You're going to make a real gutsy old lady someday," Pam said admiringly, "judging from what I just saw."

"Oh, Portia! I didn't know you had that much talent," breathed Marylou.

See what I mean about having great roommates?

Not only did they tell me I was the greatest living actress since Meryl Streep, but they were all going to the evening performance, too. And how about that for loyalty and devotion?

"Rusty Nolan is taking me," said Dee with a blush.

"I'm going with Ed Hogan," Pam said offhandedly.

"I guess you'll be going with Harvey Snelling, Marylou," I said.

Marylou looked uncomfortable. "Well...no. I won't be going with Harvey. Harvey and I have broken up."

The three of us goggled at her in disbelief.

"You've actually broken up with Harvey Snelling?" Pam croaked.

"Well, actually, he's broken up with me," Marylou admitted. "Harvey says he's afraid I've gotten much too serious about him. And since he has plans to go on to medical school and all before he can think of marriage, well, he says he doesn't want to take me out anymore."

"*You've* gotten too serious about Harvey Snelling?" said Pam incredulously. "When were you ever serious about Harvey Snelling?"

"Never," said Marylou. "I've never been serious about him. To tell you the truth, I don't even like Harvey Snelling."

"Then why..." sputtered Pam.

"I just didn't know how to turn him off," Marylou explained. "You know how I hate to hurt anyone's feelings."

"He certainly doesn't care if he hurts your feelings, though," commented Pam. "Imagine him saying you were too serious about him! What a nerd! Haven't I said all along he wasn't worthy of you?''

"Why didn't you mention it before, Marylou?" I asked.

"I didn't want to bother you. You had enough problems with Hugh and the ghost and the play."

"Well, I hope you'll come to the evening performance with Rusty and me," Dee offered.

"Thank you, Dee," Marylou said. "But actually I've got a date with Raymond Barker. He's really cute, don't you think? He told me he's been wanting to ask me out all semester, but he thought I was going steady with Harvey. So now that Harvey and I have broken up...well..."

"We might as well save our sympathy," Pam said. "Marylou doesn't need it. As long as there's a man left alive on the face of this earth, Marylou will have a date. A nuclear holocaust could destroy civilization as we know it today but somewhere, somehow, some man will struggle up from the slime and get a crush on Marylou. I can't stand it! I truly can't stand it!"

"Really, Pam," Dee said, "you do tend to overdramatize everything."

"Listen, Pam," Marylou said anxiously. "That's not so. I've stayed home dateless many a Saturday night."

"When?" Pam demanded. "When have you ever stayed home dateless on a Saturday night?"

"Well," Marylou said. "Well, let me see..."

"Never! You've never sat home on Saturday night. Admit it!"

Marylou was still vainly trying to recollect a lonely weekend when I left for the evening performance of *Our Town*.

Miss Columbo says it isn't professional to peep through the curtains at the audience before a performance, but I peeped anyway. Mom, Dad and Tess were in the front row, with Enid and Mr. Hamilton. Mr. Hamilton had his arm around Enid, and they were smiling at each other. Mr. Hamilton positively glowed, and I've never seen Enid look so beautiful. Well, as Shakespeare said, all's well that ends well.

Dee, Rusty Nolan and Dee's Aunt Edna were in the second row with Marylou and Raymond Barker. Dee and Aunt Edna were going to take Marylou home with them and drive her to Dulles airport the next morning for her flight to New York. Marylou's mother, as Lila Lamour, had to play a heavy scene the next day—her miraculous recovery from blindness—so she couldn't drive down to get Marylou. Thank God, I thought. Lila Lamour will regain her sight in time for Thanksgiving!

Pam, Ed Hogan and Pam's parents sat next to Dee and Aunt Edna. Dr. Shultz must have been telling Ed one of his proctologist jokes, because Ed was convulsed with laughter.

And in the row behind them was a couple I didn't recognize at first. Finally it dawned on me that the lady in the red satin dress and purple sequined stole was Violet, the upstairs maid. And that her date, who bore an amazing resemblance to Yves Montand, was none other than good old Antoine, the formerly sinister handyman.

Antoine must have taken my advice to heart, because he'd shaved off his beard and gotten a haircut. He was even wearing a spiffy new suit. And he was smiling. Who would have guessed it? Violet and Antoine!

In all modesty I have to admit that my evening performance was positively superb. Real star quality.

When we were all taking our fourth curtain call, it suddenly hit me.

About Raquel's hair, I mean.

What with all the excitement, I hadn't really had a chance to think it through before. Why had Raquel's hair turned green and fallen out? I certainly hadn't tinkered with her fancy French shampoo. That bottle of shampoo had been sitting in the reception room when the rest of us were in the auditorium. Not a living soul had access to it. Not a living soul. But maybe an unquiet spirit?

After the play, Mom and Dad invited Josh to dinner with us at the Horse and Hounds. He said he would get his car and meet us there. My suitcase was all packed and Tess helped me carry it out to the parking lot. Enid said she and Alan would join us later.

"Would you mind waiting a few minutes?" I asked Dad. "I have to run back to the reception room. I've, ah, forgotten something."

"Don't be too long, darling," Mom chirped. "We're all starving."

The reception room was deserted. Only one lamp was lit, and it burned dimly. I walked over to the fireplace and called softly, "Clotilde? Clotilde? Can you hear me?'' No one answered. The lamp didn't flicker or jitter on the table. Nothing.

"Clotilde?" I said again.

Gradually I became aware that my ankles were growing cold. I looked down. Perhaps it was just a trick of lighting, but I thought I saw a small patch of mist on the floor before me. I shivered.

"Clotilde?"

Still no answer.

I sighed and leaned my head wearily against the mantelpiece. The portrait of Good Queen Bess stared regally down on me. I closed my eyes. I felt tired.

"You did it, didn't you? The shampoo, I mean," I said. A gust of wind rattled in the fireplace. It sounded like ghostly laughter.

I know this sounds weird, but I felt close to Clotilde. Like a friend. I guess I always had, right from the start. It was as if she'd been watching out for me from that first night, the night at the dance, because we had something in common. The guys we'd loved had both turned out to be, well, *cochons*. But I hadn't been desperate enough to blast mine away. I'd found somebody new, somebody worth loving. And this time there'd be a happy ending. Somehow I thought that would make Clotilde happy and content. At least I hoped so.

The table lamp began to burn brighter and the mist at my feet dissipated. Perhaps it had never been there. Perhaps it had been merely a shadow. But the sensation of cold around my feet was gone. For the first time in this room I felt a pleasant warmth.

I came out of my reverie and looked around. The room seemed empty and lonely. I was still standing before the fireplace when Antoine and Violet came in.

"I think she's gone," I said.

"Who?" asked Violet. "Who's gone?"

"Clotilde?" asked Antoine. "Do you mean Clotilde?"

"Who's Clotilde?" asked Violet.

"Your grandmother said the way would be made clear," I said.

"I didn't know you knew Antoine's grandmother, honey," Violet said admiringly. "Fancy that!"

"How? How did it happen? I do not comprehend," said Antoine.

"How did what happen?" demanded Violet.

"I'm not quite sure," I answered. "I feel so strange."

"I wish someone would tell me what we're talking about," complained Violet.

Antoine smiled. He looked ten years younger and quite handsome in a French sort of way. "I think that Clotilde is gone forever."

"Clotilde who? You two are driving me crazy," said Violet.

"It is a long, sad tale, my dear Violet," Antoine said, bowing low over Violet's hand and kissing it with a courtly flourish. "One, I am sure, we shall relate many times to our grandchildren."

"Oh, Antoine!" Violet breathed. "Oh, Antoine!"

"Shall we go to dinner?" Antoine said, offering Violet his arm.

"My goodness!" Mom said as I climbed into the back seat of our car. "We thought you were never coming out. I was getting ready to go in and find you. What on earth have you been doing?"

"Saying goodbye to an old friend," I said.

We drove down the winding lane toward the Horse and Hounds, toward Josh and Enid and Alan and the future.

* * * * *

Portia and her roommates are going on a crazy vacation. Read about it in SPRING BREAK by Bebe Faas Rice, coming next month from Keepsake.

The Basic Pedicure

1. Wash your feet in the bath or in a basin of warm soapy water.

2. Soak about five minutes.

3. Work up a lather and scrub rough heel areas with a pumice stone, loofah or washcloth. Remove dead skin cells and wake skin up!

4. Dry feet thoroughly with a thick towel, especially between the toes.

5. Apply a moisturizer all over feet, especially on heels, which tend to be dry.

6. Sprinkle on a little powder or cornstarch to help stem foot odor and perspiration. (Your feet have 250,000 sweat glands and can give off as much as half a pint of perspiration a day.) But don't go overboard with the powder—pouring an entire container on your foot will cause caking and may eventually lead to infection.

7. Cut toenails straight across. Do not try to file or shape.

8. If you like, paint your toenails a fashionable color. They'll look very pretty with open-toed sandals or barefoot at the beach. Paint toenails the same way you paint fingernails.

COMING NEXT MONTH
FROM
Keepsake

COMING NEXT MONTH
FROM
CROSSWINDS™

THE HOUSE WITH THE IRON DOOR
by Margaret Mary Jensen

April was determined to find the cause of her grand-
father's mysterious death. Was the answer behind the
iron door?

FROG EYES LOVES PIG
by James Deem

At the top of Allan's list was, *Get a girlfriend*. But first he
had to change his image. It wouldn't be easy.

AVAILABLE THIS MONTH

THE BLACK ORCHID
Susan Rubin

STU'S SONG
Janice Harrell

Little extras you'll love...

In the next few months we'll be bringing you some important tips about hair, nails, makeup...everything you need to know to look good!

**How to care for your skin
Makeup do's and don'ts
The perfect hairstyle for you
Beauty quizzes...**
    and much more.

Watch for these extras from now on...
    in Keepsake and Crosswinds books.